# Notepad Stories

# Notepad *Stories*

Usha Chandrasekharan

PARTRIDGE

A Penguin Random House Company

**To order additional copies of this book, contact**
Partridge India
000 800 10062 62
orders.india@partridgepublishing.com

www.partridgepublishing.com/india

# Contents

*In the autumn of life, the trees growing tall,*
*Reaching for the skies, golden leaves pillow a fall.*

"Remembering Annaji"

# *Introduction*

A magazine keeps company as we commute. A novel, on a longer journey. These objects require your rapt attention. But, in the *'Notepad' that* you are about to read you will just flit past. Some are annoyingly less than a page. Suddenly you may doubt your judgement in browsing through the book, let alone purchase it! What is set before you is a set of stories that may not be slotted into any genre. What you read here, as an indication of what you could expect, is being done solely from my position of a Rasikan (fan).

Mystery, suspense, melodrama, satire, humour, and some more of the feelings that we pass through in our lives and trivia, yes trivia – everything is there. Luckily not tomes on each, or even short stories, but very very short notes! Seemingly notes about events as reported by a passerby from another dimension.

You will realise that the words are intricately placed in taut positioning. Quite a lot of words. Very economically & efficiently written, that, if you do not hold yourselves, the reading seems to make no sense & becomes incoherent. So, occasionally you may even be forced to read again, to make sure. Is it fiction. No, all these incidents could have happened at some place, at some time, anywhere. An object which does not need your complete attention for long periods of time. But, during the short time span of reading each article it demands total submission. At the end of reading any one 'note' you could be left with mixed feelings – one of which could be your desire to meet the author and give your piece of mind!

*Shri Naresh Kumar Nathamji*, is a conventional theme; *The Rape,* an intriguing title with a suggestively conventional expectation and the end gives you another facet of the word; *The Launch* leaves you in a slight confusion, but then it is metadrama, is it? *The Smile* is a zing thing, utterly silly, yet, it could happen! *The Irish Streak*has a naughty first para and the end leaves the disgruntled voyeur quite amused! In *Chiaroscuro* you learn another new word, a recollection finally unfolds into the harsh reality of a life's event, which could change anybody's life abruptly and also sets you thinking about certain moral issues in society. *The Fence*, as fine as an AC novel, but told so swiftly and so cuttingly, you never expected it. . . . . STOP. Nothing more from me. Read for yourselves and experience.

**Dr. N. Lakshminarayan**
**Professor in Physics,**
**Retd. From MADRAS CHRISTIAN COLLEGE,**
**Chennai, INDIA.**

# Preface

I wish I was a leadership guru. I am not. Or at least a yogi with a charmed life that I could write about. I am not. I must add, however, that my life has been enriched by the various people I have met in my life. There has been more often than not a feeling of empathetic superimposition of persona and personality. I could feel through their skin, the pain or joy of the moment. It gave me a 3-D sensation: my own reaction, the reaction of the person in front of me, and an anticipated response from some significant others in my professional life.

Every story has its own reason. Something happens; I see an end that is not what happens in real life. I at once pen it down and twist the tale in the tail. I love Jeffrey Archer for giving me this phrase. It is my mantra. After posting the stories on our group forum, I would literally lie in wait for the responses and / or critiques. I have enjoyed writing the stories I wrote. I hope people enjoy reading it as much. I shall love to get feedback from my readers.

If there is anyone reading this who wants to blame someone for authors like me, do share the blame amongst the elite few.

I am eternally grateful to:

Late Mushtaque Ali Khan Babi (Max Babi), poet, writer, and jazz expert from Pune, who pushed and prodded me to write my thoughts and poems.

Bagyam Viswanathan, my aunt, who kept faith in my writing.

Annapurani Swaminathan, my Mom, who always wanted her kids to do big.

Glory Sasikala, Moderator of the writing forum, "Glorioustimes," where I did all my thinking and creating.

All those whose critiquing helped me write my stories better and taught me to do so with precision.

My stories are also based on some crazy friends. I have used their names here, I am sure they will not mind. After all how many of you know I know them too? My favorite pastime is watching people behave and misbehave. I love long train journeys; my easel is easily filled with the vast panorama of life as it unfolds, at once quaint and unbelievable as it is happening and totally believable.

Thank you Partridge Publishers and your representatives who encouraged me to open the first pages of my book to the public.

# Meeee

I signed my name with a flourish
In college I was proud to be,
When down plunked the register
And the Dean peered at me.

"Where is the initial, the surname?"
His query seared me.
Innocently I said, "I am Monisha,
Just Monisha, don't you see?"

"Is Just your father's name?
Or that of your husband to be?"
I heard him out, there was no way,
And counted up to ten, very slowly

"Just is not my father, who is long dead and gone,
Just is not my middle name
Nor my uncle nor my husband to be!
Just is just Monisha, and Monisha is me!"

"Can you not think of a woman
On her own feet, one two or three?
Who has no man by her side, father, brother or hubby?
Is not a woman complete then without their surety?"

1

# Motherhood

Maimed, mangled,
Tied up in knots
Of self-imposed discipline
That you may crawl, toddle, ramble, walk and
Fall…fall…
Get up and run again
On your own.
Caring, praying, and believing
That in independence and freedom
You will give me your hand
Of your own accord
In acceptance and love of
Motherhood.

# Shri Naresh Kumar Nathamji

The stage was set for the biggest, most important event in industry circles. The dais looked simply elegant, with crisp white lilies in their green jackets adorning the rostrum. A beautiful selection of the best red and white roses arranged by a professional florist graced the centre table. The ceremonial lamp hastily borrowed from the Tamil Nadu Emporium gleamed delightfully in its corner. One of the overhead lights shone on it and flirtingly brought out the shining polish on the lamp to perfection.

The slightly oblong room soberly dressed for the occasion seemed to exude a charm of its own. The desultory "ullo, ullo, ullo" of the technician at the microphone resonated through the room, reflecting the wonderful acoustics in the town auditorium.

Right on the dot at six o'clock, the invited guests streamed in with their bejewelled spouses in tow. The rustle of silks and the clack of heels mingled with excited whispers of shared secrets and "excuse me please". There was an aura of pleasant anticipation as guests and hosts outshone each other in courteous exchanges of mundane pleasantries. They were gathered there that day to honour the most successful doyen of them all-Shri Naresh Kumar Nathamji.

This day, all rivalries had been set aside. The serious business of felicitation was in progress. The Chairman in his address was extolling the impressive achievements of his colleague and long-time friend, Nathamji. The august assembly was suitably captivated. One after the other, the speakers eulogized Shri Nathamji's accomplishments, shamelessly employing hyperbolic manifestation of flowery language, to create a larger than life image of Shri Nathamji.

And thus it came about that the august personage was invited to the dais to receive the award and citation. He was garlanded and honoured with the presentation of a plaque and a handsome purse. The purse would of course enhance his already brimming coffers, and the plaque would soon take pride of place of such paraphernalia on his mantelpiece at home.

The secretary in an effort to outdo his colleagues in the art of sycophancy gushed into the microphone. He called upon "the woman behind this great man" to come to the stage and be honoured too. The poor man in his haste did not mention the name of the woman he wanted on the stage. The hapless worthy was unwittingly the instigator of a war of words that threatened to cast the whole function into a state of utter confusion and embarrassment.

Two women stopped near the steps of the dais, looking daggers at each other. "You?" "How dare you?" seemed to be the unspoken words hanging between them, until a perfectly smart-witted member of the press corps, very composedly placated ruffled feathers with a garland each for the two women in Shri Nathamji's life-his mother and his secretary of twenty years standing.

# The Rape

It seemed the most logical matter for discussion. The news had spread like wildfire on a dry day. The people crowded round the tea shops were at it, nineteen to the dozen. They could not think or talk of anything else. Imagine, they seemed to say, nothing is sacred in this world. This event had taken place in the Big House. Anywhere else, it would not have made news. This happened in the Big House? Impossible!

Arati was tight-lipped. She did not want to know any more. She was thoroughly disgusted with the whole affair and the unnecessary public airing it was receiving. She had taken care to explain to the children how they were expected to behave in polite society. Noblesse Oblige was part and parcel of her upbringing. She thought she had transmitted all her learning to her own children and the children in her extended family. She waited in dread for the return of her husband and father-in-law from their business trip. How would they respond and react to all the brouhaha going on?

She sat down wearily in her chair by the window. The happenings of the last week ran through her mind like a cinema trailer. Her father-in-law's business demanded a lot of travel and high level meetings in different countries all over the world. Quite recently, after a minor heart attack at a sales seminar in their Mumbai unit, Rahul had taken to accompanying him on his tours. If only he had been here, he would have handled the situation with discretion and aplomb. Whatever her grouses were about him, she knew her husband was extremely dependable and prudent.

The day it all began, she had found the subtle difference in the atmosphere in the room disturbing. She could not place the cause of the discomfort. The children seemed to be sharing some secret amongst themselves. The sudden silences neatly filled with catchy movie songs by the older kids and the furtive kicks under the table had not escaped her silent vigilance. She only wished she had been more alert and had intruded into their domain with greater resolution. Her need to show trust in the children was definitely a motive for not barging into their privacy. How else could she ensure their continued faith in her? She had prayed fervently that nothing untoward was being planned or happening. After the news broke, she thought sadly that her prayers had not only gone unanswered but had also been smashed to smithereens.

The violent ringing of the doorbell snatched her out of her reverie. She shuddered to her feet, delaying the moment of meeting or interacting with her in law. She had to face things, anyway. Covering her head with her stole, Arati opened the door and silently made way for them to enter the house. Her father- in- law was looking serious and she worried that he may have already heard about it. In great trepidation she played her role of gracious hostess, offering them tea and snacks before getting the dinner going.

She caught her husband's eye and conveyed a silent instruction to him. He followed her into the kitchen and raised his eyes in a query. "What is it? Dad had another episode of heartburn. He is not too well," he told her quietly. In agony, she said, "the children Ashia and Sheen had been rummaging in his room. They found a red diary and had been reading it. When Dilip uncle went to see what was going on in the room, the kids threw the book out of the window. Unfortunately the schoolmaster's second son who we all know, is a ruffian got hold of it and has been talking of its contents to all the village folk. What could I do? I have been pretending that the book does not belong to us at all..." Her distress petered into an uneasy silence.

The thudding sound at the kitchen door had both of them wheeling around to see her father- in- law squirming in a different kind of pain. He had overheard her! "My God! What have they done? My red diary contained all my private observations about our family, their strengths and weaknesses; their foibles and fallacies. Oh my God! All our family secrets that should never have seen the light of day are now public knowledge. The whole village knows about us now. How will I face any of the family? Life will never be the same again." Clutching his chest in agony, he eased painfully out of his trauma. Life was never the same again. Their collective privacy had been thrown open to the world. Like the aftermath of a hurrying hurricane, each and everyone was affected, blemished, and laid bare like a specimen on the dissecting table. The rape was complete.

# Nelson Ishwar Das

Nelson Ishwar Das went into his two- room house at the end of Priya Ranjan Das Street after his day's work. He was a guard at the nearby shrimp processing factory when he was not busy with the government duties. Nishda, as he was more popularly known, took himself very seriously indeed, as he did his daily routine. This was his Karma and his Dharma. He brooked no interference from anyone, friend or foe.

Early every morning, before the world woke up, he would be on his way to the small courtyard at the back of the house. After his morning ablutions and a bath in the cold water from the pump set there, he would spend an hour in prayer. Meditation followed, which in his case, was a low rumbling recanting of some unintelligible mantra muttered with a swaying of his upper torso, from back to front. His guru, the one who had talked to him about Dharma and who had cleansed his mind of all lingering doubts about his ability to go to heaven in his afterlife, had shown him how. While he meditated, he remembered all the people who had passed through his hands, and he humbly asked for their forgiveness. He asked them to bless his family, especially his son who would take over his work when he retired. Then he set about getting his apparatus ready. The long jute rope, of a thickness specified by the government, was checked and tested every day for readiness. He could not allow it to be frayed, not even the smaller rope with its thinner ply. Its quality could never be faulted. The black sack like apparel, stitched with great care was made of hundred counts of the best cotton both in the weave and the weft. He also checked to see if he had a copy of The Gita, Koran, and The Bible in mint condition. One never knew which one would be needed.

Only after he went through this self- imposed inspection of the tools of his trade, would he let himself partake of a frugal but healthy breakfast. After more than three years, he was due for one more call at the Central Prison, that day. This time around it was a young man in his late thirties. Youthful arrogance coupled with a few swigs of neat whisky had empowered him to take the life of two young women in his employment, who had dared to refuse his lustful advances. Nelson Ishwar Das was ready to do his duty as Official Hangman for the State. This was his Dharma and his Karma.

# *The Launch*

The stage was set, the participants present in their formal best, and the turnout was excellent for a function arranged in a short time. It was to be a great event in their lives. Hari and Haritha ventured timidly into the hall. As they tiptoed to the damask covered round tables designated for them, they held hands and smiled nervously at each other. All around them, the last minute hustle and bustle went on unmindful of their duress. The low stage had on one end a narrow rostrum for a speaker, and was well decorated.

Photos of a handsome young man, rather well filled out and stout looked askance at their discomfiture. They were placed at flattering intervals and seemed to bolster their waning confidence. His round red face reflecting the heat from the oven at which he was working, showed up the spark of creativity igniting his eyes. They smiled happily through anxious eyes at the beloved face and at each other. "I am sure it will go well. Do not worry," said Hari, as he gently flattened her bunching knuckles on the table.

They had prepared well for this day. Nirmal had tutored them in all the nuances of fine dining. He wanted them to know the basics even though he knew he would not mind if they did not use all he had taught. They lapped up all the instructions and practiced at home. Both were determined not to let their celebrity son down, that too on the eve of such a big event being organized to showcase his talents. Haritha had already propitiated all her favourite gods for the success of his event. They had even prepared their paunch lines.

The speeches were made, medals given, and certificates distributed. The much awaited launch was announced officially, with the paparazzi hustling each other to get the best pictures. All present watched with bated breath as the entrees were brought in by liveried waiters carrying in huge soup tureens. The starters and appetizing nibbles of mushroom and cauliflower fritters were met with satisfied sighs of 'oohs' and 'aahs'. The main course was temptingly dressed with stuffed potatoes and juicy kebabs dripping the goodness of clarified butter. The saffron colored biryani was accompanied by a duet of side dishes. The sweet syrupy papaya chutney vied for attention with the red hot peppers and onions sautéed in a secret herbal aroma. Without doubt, the dessert of piping hot banana fries served on extra cold butterscotch ice-cream was the best.

The launch ended with thunderous applause, as the chef, Nirmal Hari, came up on stage to accept the accolades of the dignitaries present. Haritha had tears in her eyes as she beamed at her son along with her husband. Sentiment caused many a wet eye as the parents looked on accepting humbly the standing ovation being accorded to their son.

"Where is that sub- editor of mine?" yelled a voice, as young Bob raced to answer the summons. "Bob, dear Bob, your spell check has let you down again. See, every Launch has to be made into 'LUNCH', understand? The 'PAUNCH' is 'PUNCH'. Got that?" the voice bellowed, as Bob got busy editing the story of The Lunch.

# The Shadows on the Ceiling

Nirmala Kakima (aunt) looked up at the ceiling with great concentration. She seemed deep in thought. Her gnarled old hands that bespoke years of an active working life held each other in empathetic support. God knew how many times she had wrung those very hands in despair or in prayer. Today they seemed to be having emotions of their own. The bereaved family watched.

Nirmala Kakima took the photograph in her hands and looked at it. It seemed to be demanding some kind of justice from her. It was a police photo, a copy of the original that had been enlarged a few times. It was very clear. She traced the salty trail extending from the corner of the left eye through the crags and pain lines that reached the corner of the mouth and stopped there. Had he in his last moments swallowed his tears? The bereaved family watched.

Tabola had always been a cheerful and quick learner. He was neat. He had kept house for her all these years without a single day of argument or resentment at the excessive workload when her family visited. She had had to visit her brother in hospital a long way away. She had left him in charge of the house, promising to come back in three days. All this had happened in her absence. She shifted position in her armchair and looked at them. The bereaved family looked back, watching her.

Nirmala looked hard at the photograph, fighting the urge to cry aloud and throw up. She had had a soft corner for this chap. He had been very loyal to her. He would always go the extra mile to see her comfortable. There were servants and servants. Tabola had been a great asset; the best of them all. Now this issue faced her. Some vague memory stirred her memory. She sat up with a start as she recollected what it was.

Taking the photograph to the light she breathed deeply to steady her raging emotions. She looked at the patient group near the door. They sat quietly and watched her. They knew she was a just woman. She would tell them what to do. She would be ready to expose the police if need be. They trusted her. They knew he had not hanged himself. They knew that their son would not cry. They knew he was not a coward. They just waited and watched.

Sitting in her armchair she looked up at the ceiling. It was nearing eleven on the kitchen clock. She looked at the two kitchen windows placed at the extreme end of two adjacent walls. They were not exactly opposite each other but the positioning did duty toward cross ventilation. She looked upward as the bright stream of sunlight played with the light fittings and the wires, creating the special double shadow effect on the ceiling. Sharp at eleven the shadow of the bulb could be seen on both sides of the reaper carrying the wires. This sight used to fascinate her before. She looked at the photograph that had a clock showing the time in the background as eleven o'clock. She picked up the phone and called the commissioner of police.

The family of Tabola sensed the change in her purpose-filled demeanour and her stance. Now they had anticipation in their eyes as they sat and watched her.

The time was ten thirty. The commissioner had said he would be on time. He was. He was punctual. She was curt and businesslike. She was a powerful woman and influential. The corridors of power shivered when she pointed an accusing finger at anyone. She showed him the police photograph, pointed to the time on the clock placed in the background, and the ceiling in the photo. She showed him the shadows on the ceiling at eleven in the morning in the kitchen. He did not die here. Your photo lies. The clock was adjusted to show a different time. Where are the shadows? The body was hanged here post mortem. Your force lies. Give us the truth. She looked at the waiting family of Tabola. "Go and find the truth from him," she said, as the menacing terrorizing group advanced on the helpless, turned- to -jelly chief of police.

# The Smile

The smile lingered. It encompassed all who saw with its beauty. It lit up the eyes above, causing a slight twinkle to appear. The twinkle added lustre to the face. A small dimple began its journey on a bristly chin and soon covered more space, lighting up the whole face. Could a small smile really do all that? It did, and more.

The smile enlivened the surroundings, causing some flutters. It brought an answering mirror- like response from the rest of the room. The electrifying bonhomie created an awareness of joy and camaraderie. Even the shyest reader seemed to bask in the glow spread by the slightly expanded zygomatic muscles on the handsome face. The look of spreading kindliness, we ascribed to a loving wife's culinary expertise. But no, he denied with a strong shake of his head. It was the poetry meet; his shaking head seemed to say.

The poets, published or otherwise, stood before the audience and recited their works of art, carefully crafted and more carefully presented. What added to the individual's performance, however, was the gentle countenance of the smiling organizer. He seemed to exude a strong feeling of reassurance. Even the youngest at age seven and the oldest at age eighty three reflected the calm confidence born of an acceptance twinkling out of a pair of star lit eyes. Each person there struck a comfortable pose in spite of publicly revealing his/her soul for the first time.

They willingly accepted his critiques and gentle humour at their expense. All the adulation was, however, not directed to his work or sense of humour. It was fully dedicated to the pair of dark orbed brilliance brightly lit by the bow shaped smile that tenderly included each and every participant in its ambit. Each one was egged on to a better performance and a promise of more prolific output for the next read meet of the Glorious Times group.

And then he turned back to look at me, cowering in the corner. His smile still in place, his eyes turned to a hard glassy stare. I shivered. I had every reason to be mortally afraid of him. I read the threat in the smile plastered to his face. I was tethered to the chair by the legs under the cover of my lovely Kanchipuram sari, which I had worn just for this occasion. If the brute had his way, I would not be wearing it anymore after this day.

*I had chanced upon his diary on the steps to the auditorium. In picking it up to see to whom it belonged, the book fell out of my hands and opened at the first page, revealing that it was not a book at all. The pages had been sealed, and an aperture cut into the top. This now held a tiny but effective looking explosive in place. I had looked up to see him studying my face. He had held out his hand and quietly gestured me toward the chair in the back of the hall. The setting off device was in his hands. He looked diabolic and I feared for my life. I had learned he*

*meant to blow up the hall just as the chief guest was leaving.*
*How could I do anything? What could I do?*

He must have read my thoughts from across the room, for I saw him write something on a piece of paper and pass it to me through a young girl. I shuddered in morbid expectation as I opened it to read two words APRIL FOOL on it. When I looked up again, THE SMILE had become a huge big beam of uncontrolled mirth and sent the whole gathering into peals of laughter as he recounted the story behind his SMILE.

# In Alicia's Land

How intensely he loved to please, showed in the many errands he ran for her, however irksome or childish. He sat long hours with her when she was sick, helped in the kitchen when there were guests. Sometimes he even washed the toilets after they had left. He did not think it wrong to work in this manner. His father would have been very irritated, he knew. This work was his own choice and he stood by it for whatever it was worth.

He had schooled his features not to show revulsion for any of the smelly jobs. He had perfected the art of getting the servants to do the dirty work most of the time, and then he would sail in at the appropriate moment to claim the honours. He was a survivor, not like his fond parent up above, he told himself as he searched the heavens for some sign that the old man knew and understood. He had an agenda and was working toward its successful culmination. Until then... he could wait. He would wait. He would have to wait.

Time whiled away life in other pursuits. She became restless and called more frequently upon him to entertain her. This he did willingly and unstintingly. Her alabaster skin looked translucent in the shaded light of a hot Indian summer afternoon, as he busied himself with the board game of Chinese checkers that she loved to play. Theirs was an easy relationship and neither had to pretend to win or lose. She won some and lost some, her eyes wandering to the clock on the shelf willing it to move faster. After the game, both decided to read aloud from her favourite book of Bible stories. They took to discussing and arguing about the merits and demerits of the protagonists of the stories. This allowed night to sneak in on them without much ado. One more day had been lived through with relative ease.

He had to put her through the paces of the exercises that the physiotherapist had entrusted him with. She was mostly cooperative but there were days and days! Sometimes he wished he had not started on this venture at all. But when she was willing, the experience was very pleasurable and both lingered on in appreciative contemplation. Or so he thought. He mused on her beautiful soft skin. The shy pink colour that suffused her cheeks brought him back to the present with a bang. She must not get any wrong ideas about his intentions. Brusquely, he requested her to turn over so that he could continue with his ministrations. This was the difficult part as her legs just could not be bent backwards without hurting her. At last it was all over and he could leave her to relax with her customary glass of warm milk.

In another day and time, life would have been so different. He remembered snatches of sequences from some lovely movies he had seen in the past. Especially the royal romances had caught his fancy and stayed to colour his present day existence. He recalled the daring escapades of Princess Diana and the other lady whose name he could not bring to mind. Both had lived such exciting lives. They had loved their fast cars and wild adventurous sorties to taste the addictive but forbidden fruits of Eden. His imagination kindled, he stayed glued to his easy chair and his thoughts till sleep took over.

He had researched well and compounded the mixtures as per specifications. He helped her with spreading the paste on her face and the long nape of her neck. He covered every inch of exposed skin with the diligence of a new intern. He would wash it off in a short while and leave Alicia to ask of her mirror if she was truly fairer than before. While he waited for the paste to dry, he would colour her nails and do a bit of pedicure too. She was immensely happy with his service and told him so. He collected these credits in the mandatory forms and carefully filed them. He would need their references later. No one he had worked on could ever testify that he practiced euthanasia. He lulled his patients into a deep sense of trust, and when he felt it right, he helped the terminally ill ones in his care to move on

# My Point of View

I had seen her somewhere before. I was sure. I could not, however, place the time or date of my having seen her. I looked into her eyes whenever I could. I stared into her soul seemingly, for she would fidget uncomfortably. Sometimes the cup in the saucer held out by her would clatter. Not a big noise mind you, but enough to cause me to look down at it. The moment I stopped looking at her, she was robust, gaily cheerful, and full of bonhomie. Her loud chatter permeated my very system forcing me to get on with the job of waking up to a new day.

Breakfast was a chore. The cook was slovenly. She never seemed to register my tastes or preferences. Either there was too much oil or too little. Oil rich food was invariably hidden under an overdose of bread crumbs or flour or sometimes even an overkill of tomato puree. I hated the red of the tomatoes in the curried accompaniment to the toasted bread. How much tastier and simpler bread and butter was with a jar of good jam for licking off dripping fingers? This woman would never accept my menu. I ended up throwing as much of the food as possible. I had my point of view and could not eat happily if I did not get exactly as I asked. She would look at me in fear when I threw food around. How easy it was to frighten her I thought and felt my power.

I hated to go out. I hated crowds. Especially, when they looked at me in assessment, I could feel their thoughts creeping over my skin and into my body through the pores. I preferred to sit at home on the swing or in the rocking chair. Rocking to and fro has such a serene feeling to it. I could rock on and on. Even sitting on a chair I could rock for ages if the woman allowed me. If she saw me rocking she would come at a fast trot and try to change my seat. What a bore she was. One day I told myself I would force her to do all the things she was forcing me to do now. Who was she? I keep thinking I have met her before but....where?

Why did she not ever leave me alone to do what I wanted? I constantly brooded over this mystery and the answer eluded me. The young man with short hair standing in a frizzle loved it when I called him Sonny. He would jump up at that call like Tim Tom my pet spaniel. Sonny was special. He would never hurt me. He agreed wholeheartedly to seek the wicked neighbours hiding behind the hedge. They disturbed my sleep with loud arguments and would not go if I yelled at them. Sonny had to only go near them and speak in a low voice and they would go away. After that, I would sleep only if Sonny promised to sit with me. His nice, soft hands patting my cheeks were a great comfort. He would read from his books stories that I never understood but which I pretended to enjoy. It gave him great pleasure to be with me and I loved it too. He was not like the others. I could trust him.

The other day the poor thing had come into the room with a lot of blood on his face. Someone had scratched him. I fainted on seeing the blood. He never came near me after that. He would stand some way away and talk to me as if he was afraid. Why was he afraid of me? I do not know. I miss his soft caresses. That woman screamed at me when I asked about Sonny. I am tired. I want to sleep. The noises won't go away. Sonny won't come to me. Tim Tom does not like to be held close to me when I sleep. He keeps wriggling and runs away. I do not like my food. I do not like anything anymore. That man on television was saying "If you do not like anything anymore, just cut your wrist, and tomato sauce will flow." I know he said it even if that woman says he did not.

Why am I tied up like this? What is this bandage on my hand? Who is this rough man standing near the bed? No I do not want to eat. I do not want to bathe. Leave me alone. Leave me alone. I only want Sonny boy. I want to rock with him on my lap. Sonny, Sonny where are you my boy? That woman called me names. She said I was a stupid schizoid. Sonny, tell her to go. Go Go. This is my life. I am not a Schizoid. I am not. Sonnnny!

# The Irish Streak

"Got it?" "Yes. Somewhat". "Just remember the rules. No Streaks outside the Irish Border. Get proof of location and time on the photos. Do not ask me how. The how of it all is your problem. I only want the photos. The best exposures, you know, get the prize money and the "Blue" Film Society Ribbon. Okay guys, on your way!" Sharmila waved her companions away on their leather hunt for the best shot.

The film society awards were an annual event that drew crowds of participants from all over the world. This time too, there were at least nine clubs from India taking part. She had to do a lot of research on the award categories, the mindset of the judges, the norms for the photo-shoots, and the kind of shots that would get them high points in each of the sub-divisions that would get them the prize. She was a professional. There was no doubt about the way she went about her role as the chief adviser for the film club. She made sure that the teams had the best cameras and trained them in the art of outdoor photography. After all one can't shoot a streak inside a room, she grinned naughtily.

The three teams that she had formed had the right mix of members. Team A was the most mature of the lot. She had high hopes for them. Jason was a natural. He knew the subject well, was patient, ready for the unexpected and truly dependable. He was the unofficial reference point for the others. He would also be handling all the officials when they went over to Ireland. He was the best person she knew who would cajole their shy models into revealing more than the norm. His was the most delicate job of all. She had faith in his abilities and sat back in her high chair at the conference table, full of hope of bagging the prize.

Squeals of delight and shrieks of congratulations rent the normally placid atmosphere of the conference room. The fruits of their labour were laid out in order on the table, neatly labelled. Sharmila was grinning like the proverbial Cheshire cat that had already tasted the cream. Each of the exposures was superbly done. All her teams had done well and now were in the process of selecting the best for a collage of their work. The slides for the power point presentation drew more exclamations of "great!" from the whole team. The best streaks were displayed in a separate template with the name age and sex of the model typed in bold. This one was the shyest he reminisced, and this was his best shot.

Sharmila began her presentation in front of the judges, made up of the country's best lepidopterists, wildlife experts, lepidopterologists, and editors of wildlife magazines. This she declared triumphantly, is the Irish Streak, identified by the streak of white on its normally brown or buff forewings. The scientific name is Chesias Legatella, and belongs to the Geometrid family." On and on she went, describing the best streak they could ever hope to see.

# Stoned

The ripples on the surface of the small pond shivered and shuddered. The bigger ones quickly rushed in to hide the smaller ones and covered their secret shame. They slowly stopped all movement and let nature work its way in their depths.

Shanmugha Sundaram sat on the pitted moss-covered bricks built around the ancient well and ruminated on his life. His position as a member of the local panchayat kept him gainfully occupied. He wondered how old people spent their lives after retirement. He could not imagine himself sitting idle, gossiping, or spitting well chewed betel leaves into huge spit pots. He did not think it was any kind of useful work.

He counted on his fingers all the seniors he knew and mentally granted points to those he thought were busy workers. Of course, the ancient hag, Muniamma, was his favourite. She was forever involved in decisions being taken in each and every household in the village. She knew the history of every family there. Nothing passed unnoticed by her sharp and piercing eyes. If, however, she missed something she would wheedle it out of the local gossips in a matter of seconds. By the same token, if a secret had to be kept, she was again the only one who could guard it.

Shanmugha Sundaram's vigil lasted all of five hours. He really did not have much to do as all the work was being handled by his family. He had been given an unexpected day off thanks to the viral fever that had plagued him the day before. Some stray thoughts bothered him. Last evening, his friend had mentioned carefully that his sister Sakku was being sent to her grandmother's place a few hundred miles away. It seemed that she had come of marriageable age. Being different, and disabled, having her stay at home would bring bad luck to the family. Hence, she would not be allowed to stay in the village. He had liked the kid in his own way, and felt disturbed that he would not see her for long. He knew his own sister, Seetha, too had crossed that age. No suitors had come forward to marry her. The elders were murmuring their displeasure. Would she too be packed off? Crazy customs!

A huff and puff distracted him from his musings. Why! There was Muniamma trudging up the slope to the pond on the other side of the path. She was closely followed by a well-dressed Seetha, with her yellow nylon half-sari wrapped tightly round her skinny arms. She seemed to be carrying a big stone. It looked more like the grinding stone at home. Sundaram looked on with interest as the old one waved her on to hurry. They climbed over the ridge and disappeared from view. He sat there trying to guess what they were doing at the pond. Soon enough, he saw Muniamma returning. There was no sign of the young one.

Shanmugha Sundaram called out to the senior in his usual bantering tone and asked her what she was doing. She called back crisply, "What else can I do near a pond, silly fellow?" and went her way. But where was Seetha? He climbed over the ridge and was just in time to see the bigger ripples rushing the smaller ones into covering the shameful secrets that it held.

# The Soul

"The soul is experienced through knowledge (gnan), vision (darshan), conduct (charitra), and penance (tapa). In this body, that which is mechanical, that part which is changing, is not the soul. That which is absolutely still, is in reality the soul. The one who eats, drinks, reads, meditates, etc., is purely mechanical, and not really the soul. In fact the soul is The Self, the Absolute Lord."

Chitra lay back on the bed and reflected on these words as they rose over the static of an age-old radio on her bedside table. She resented the speaker's use of the masculine singular that was used to represent the Soul. "Lord indeed!", she thought with a toss of her pretty curled head and suddenly burst into peals of laughter as she saw her husband's supine form on the lawn swing. "That which is absolutely still is the soul, the absolute Lord, "she told herself, "and there he is in the garden". The cynic in her took over and she fell in a brown study of the vastly mundane existence she was leading.

Would life ever mean more than three meals, unending washing, and interminable attention to details to make everyone's life bearable? Who am I? Why am I born? What is the purpose of my existence? Will I ever know? What is it that makes a person tick? Why do we live the way we do? What is this existence meant to achieve? Would Sachin's runs have more value to the viewer of the game than to himself? Does it really matter in the end if X won the election or Y? What if Doomsday came on at an unexpected moment, perhaps five years earlier? She finally gave up on her line of reasoning and went off to sleep.

Her energizing forty winks ended in a fresh spate of housework. She ruefully wondered what had happened to the livewire unionist she had been at college. Where were her pledges, heartfelt promises, and endless enthusiasm for oratory? These days, instructing the maid on her work for the day left her tired and frustrated. That worthy seemed to have been born in this world just to sponge on her and get well-paid holidays. Listlessly, she got into the bathroom and studied her reflection in the mirror. The apparition that greeted her had no semblance to the person she thought she was; nor to the person she had been; nor to the person she had thought she would become in the future.

Is this my soul then? She went absolutely still for a moment, lost in an introspection that rent her conscience, owned her weaknesses, took stock of her strengths, counted her blessings, and emerged fully rejuvenated. The subdued ring of the doorbell in the hall shook her out of her preoccupations and carried her hurriedly to the front door. Her mother-in-law stood there with a bag full of wool in her hand and an extremely woebegone expression on her face. "I lost my purse on the way and need to pay the auto rickshaw driver," she said forlornly.

Having taken care of her immediate needs, she sat the older woman on the comfortable sofa in the living room and listened to all her woes with an air of great concern. Together, they sorted out the knots as they talked, and Chitra helped to rewind the wool on an old clothes hanger. At the end of her long-winded account of her misadventure of the morning, she told her daughter-in-law, "You know Chitra, I think God brought you into my world because He knew I would need you. Bless you child for being so generous with your time and attention. What more can an old woman like me want?" Her eyes were wet with unshed tears that sparkled in the radiance reflected from the younger one's eyes. Chitra seemed to have found a new value for her life. There was a spring to her step as she re-entered the kitchen.

It is easy to make or break a person's faith, isn't it?

# Surprise

Casting caution to the winds, Malathi hissed loudly at the boy in the corner. The diminutive creature wearing naught but a torn khaki pant looked back askance. Typical of his ilk, he did not question the hiss. He only wanted to know why she hissed. He called back a question as he shuffled himself into a more comfortable portion of his raiment.

Malathi beckoned him to where she was standing. When he was close enough, she whispered theatrically. "Will you do a small job for me?""I will pay you," she added for good measure. The young one needed no more encouragement. He nodded happily, and in the style of his favourite matinee idol, he whisked a nonexistent lock of hair over the left part of his forehead and announced, "As soon as you express your wish, it will be done." He smiled enchantingly.

She looked backward into the dark reaches of the long corridor that formed the main living area of her house, praying that no one had seen her. "Do you see that house in the corner, the one with a reddish paint and broken step?" He nodded patiently. "Go fast, look and tell me if there is a lady there, on the swing in front of the house. Tell her, eight in the evening," she exhorted.

Quick as a flash, the kid was gone. Malathi blinked, wondering at his speed. He ran back before she could even say, "Jack Robinson." Panting, he told her that there indeed was a tall, thin girl sitting on the swing. "She was reading a book. I gave her your message. She gave me this," he added, showing her a five rupee coin. Eyes glinting at the thought of the money he was promised, he waited patiently. Laughing softly, Malathi gave him a similar coin and the brat ran away.

The rest of the day went by in a whirl of expectation; in a fever of anticipation; in a dizzy rush of plans. Malathi had arranged and re-arranged the drawing room furniture so many times, her parents eyed her warily. She had called her brother at least twenty times to tell him to be home just before eight and to be sure to bring home some of the best samosas and mint chutney from the sweet shop near his office. She herself had made a fresh batch of sugar-coated banana fritters. The house had a lovely welcoming feel about it. "All this for an old friend?" her mother's looks seemed to query.

Promptly at eight, the doorbell rang and Malathi ran to open it. Her brother stood there with a sheepish grin, apologizing for the delay in his coming. She bid him come in, looking over his shoulder to see if her guest had also come. And then, there she was!

A tall and stately lady was being escorted into the house by the brat of the morning. She stopped hesitantly near the main door, looking deeply at and into Malathi's mother's face.

Her trance was broken by an exuberant Malathi running to her with open arms. "You are at the right place, Aunt Sheela!" she said with a lot of love in her voice. Her mother was mumbling incoherently, shocked disbelief, love, sorrow, and a host of emotions gambolling on her lined features."My kid sister, Sheela, is this really you? How? Where?" Saying which, she slid slowly down onto the sofa in a happy swoon.

Malathi happily munched away on the savouries and sweets, seeing that her family was busy with the newcomer's tale of how she was looked after by a foster family for about ten years after she had been lost at an exhibition ground. She related too, the story of her life till then, and of how Malathi had tracked her through face book, and other Internet sources. A lovely surprise for the New Year, her mother looked at her daughter lovingly and gratefully.

# The Conductor

He loved his job. There were no two opinions on the issue. There was a well-scrubbed look of joyous anticipation about him as he left home every day. He seemed to derive a lot of satisfaction from what he did. His shoes shone with the "spit and polish" routine that he subjected them to, every morning. He met his mother's disgusted looks with a warm smile that melted her poor heart in a jiffy. His good mood spilled over to the people he wished with a "a very good morning" as he raced out of the house.

Every day was as different as could be. But he had his regulars. As he took charge of his "territory," as he loved to call it, his eyes fell on kindly old Katie who did the odd jobs for the self-made industrialist in town. She loved her work, and loved music more. They shared this common interest that made them friends for life. He made it a point to reserve the best seats for her. She also took it upon herself to help him out when there was a crowd that needed handling. Her strong stentorian voice had its uses, however trivial.

The chubby rosy-cheeked school boy and his young friend who accompanied him everywhere were a treat with their winsome ways. Genteel, to be sure, he told himself. Glen, as she was named, was a neighbour who loved her young friend

George with a sisterly devotion that would put most siblings to shame. Hari, a young Indian student was attending university, doing his Masters in Sociology. He had a rare voice indeed, which he trained and developed under the French Pastor who lived downtown.

Thus it was that Peter found himself gazing with great love at the people who composed his domain. Throwing off his snow-drenched leather long coat and straightening his back, he prepared himself for the arduous journey ahead. They were in their seats, attentive to every minute movement of the waving batons in his hands, a compliment to his driving magnetic qualities. Their adoration for him was there in the slight slant of their heads toward him, in the sheer concentration of their capacities as the chorale stepped up practice on their choral ensemble. Conducting a Capella was no mean issue, and he was determined to do justice to his young choristers, who depended on him to lead and win the inter-church competition in December.

# The Blank Page

The blank page whispered with the wind. It beckoned enticingly, furling and unfurling its pristine whiteness, urging her to pick up her pen and write. Her black ink fountain pen looked forlornly about. He realized he was wasted till someone waved him either as a sword or as a pen. He knew if he were used, his life would become history. But then, that was the purpose of his being, and having to wait for his time to come was becoming difficult.

She looked on pensively at the fluttering paper and the sad looking pen. What was it urging her to do? Could she really write the truth? Would there be acceptance or would she have to defend her stand? The burden of knowing the whole story had taken its toll. Her eyes looked sunk into a deep depression. Her normally robust complexion looked ready for a touch of rouge. Her sky blue outfit only accentuated the paleness of her face. Meanwhile, the clean unwritten oblong in front of her clamoured for attention. Could she soil the page with her knowledge? Dared she?

Life had never been easy. Giving tuition to stretch her meagre pocket money had strengthened her in many ways. She had learnt patience and the joy of awaiting rewards. She had learned to budget her income and her expenses. It had helped her in her first job when she had to manage the till whenever the shop owner had to step out. Her integrity shone in her eyes; People loved and trusted her and she was the toast of the little community she lived in.

It was in the house of the landlord of the local inn that she had first seen what she had seen. She had not understood what was afoot and was on the verge of yelling out for help when she heard the giggles and understood that nothing bad was happening. Somebody was having innocent fun she presumed and turned away. The second time, however, she was more intrigued. She was curious too. In fact, curiosity was her first reaction. Though tempered with a bit of prudence, her native feeling was one of curiosity. She had to know more. She wanted to be able to giggle too. She wanted to know what caused those giggles.

That brought her to the next step of the whole issue. She started stalking the gigglers to know at what the times they came to the inn. She noticed with some alarm that they came in by the backdoor, with the tacit knowledge of the cook. That worthy only winked and turned his back on the interlopers. She could not believe her eyes. About half an hour later she could hear the giggles. It was louder than before. After all, the landlord was expected to be late. She could not believe her ears. There were loud stage whispers of "bang her, bang her "and then a small weak moan, which slowly rose to a higher pitch. All at once they broke into huge giggles that got carried like a virus to the kitchen where the chef seemed to have painted a perpetual silly grin on his face.

Quietly she slipped in behind the kitchen door and entered the basement below where all the excitement had expended itself. With ill-concealed haste and eagerness she looked around. Everything seemed so normal and commonplace. What could have been the cause of all that merriment? She wished she could go and openly ask. She cursed herself for her diffidence. Tired out and disgruntled, she sat down on the settee, only to jump up in dismay as a moaning sound started below her. With a thudding heart, she looked down under the cushion to see a painted plastic face contorted in a moue of disdain at her ignorance. Clutching wildly to her sanity, she rushed out to the driveway, and thence to her room in the cottage behind the hotel.

She felt weak and tired. Even now she was not sure what she had seen, but the feeling of disgust at her own stupid investigations was uppermost in her mind. She could not stomach the fear that the gigglers may have been abusing poor "painted face" below stairs. Could she effect an escape for the victim? No she decided. She did not have the guts. She threw open the window to let in the cool evening air that would hopefully clear her head of the cobwebs gathered there, while the fluttering invitation to write flapped happily in the breeze.

She watched idly, wondering if she could talk to him. The innkeeper had arrived from his perambulations. With him was a pair of very boisterous kids, probably his grandchildren. He called to the maid to get something from inside the house. In the meantime, he set up a folding table in the front yard, covered with a checked cotton tablecloth.

He instructed his young wards to stand before the table with their eyes closed, which they could open only on his say-so. There were huge squeals of delight when they could see their presents; two huge inflated plastic dolls with vividly painted faces, which moaned realistically when they were banged. She slid silently to the floor, limp with relief.

# Power

Power was in the air. It seeped out of the thick black frames that housed the portraits of his parents and those of other assorted ancestors. It shone in the brightness of the copper vessels and plates kept in the centre of the room. It hung from the green painted beams that had held the ceiling in place for as long as the village could remember. It flared the nostrils of the scion of the family as he oversaw the preparations being made for the ceremonies. The three-inch thick kitchen door was kept assiduously shut, reining in the powerful smells rising out of the boiling cauldrons from entering the main rooms. It infused the visitors present, filling the less experienced among them with a nameless dread.

The day was auspicious. A memorial service was in progress, with a lot of Brahmans from the area having gathered to carry out the rituals. They were freshly bathed, wearing the brand new raiment given to them for the occasion. They were of all ages and earned different wages depending on their age and knowledge. The more learned flaunted their learning in the depth of the resonance as they chanted the mantras. The hollowness of the less learned could be easily made out in the shallow responses and half swallowed words. A student of human nature, Pannaiah Parameswaran noted all this as he went about his filial duties.

The day was just getting warmer as the rites came to an end on cue. Even Time, the old rascal, seemed to succumb to the sense of power in this house. The ceremonial plantain leaves were laid out with wooden planks for the pundits to sit on in front of them. The polished silver tumblers brimmed with warm water, a strong flavour of cardamom, and dried ginger tickled the senses. The huge kitchen doors were thrown open and in streamed the ladies of the house in traditional attire, carrying small service buckets and proceeded to serve the food. The smell of onions and garlic tempered with various spices filled the air, exciting the palates of the hungry men sitting cross-legged at the banquet.

Not a single protest was heard. Not even one learned voice was raised to object to the menu, which was not normally served on a day as auspicious as a memorial ritual for the dead members of a family. Some heads hung in shame. They did not dare to question their wealthy patron. All the rituals for the function had been violated. Now they were being forced to eat food that was not kosher. None of them dared to object. Power had ways of making its presence felt, and this was one. Power chose to dictate. The meek in spirit obeyed. They would live to see another day.

The various tones of disturbed emotions slowly left the powerfully august presence of Pannaiah Parmeswaran who had once more established the Power of his Pelf. Power leaned back in the royal easy chair and gloated.

# Chiaroscuro

The sun-dappled chiaroscuro on the wall filled Sachin with a deep sense of satisfaction. The play of light through the window made a pretty picturesque 'curtain'. It took him back to the house of his grandparents in the village, which now seemed so far away. There, every veranda or window seemed to create its own pattern. Each had a life of its own; changing with the slow morphing of time from morning to evening.

He remembered again the other such pictures he had seen. The one in his college hostel room used to be remarkably fluid in its features. Clothes, T-shirts, caps, and sometimes even umbrellas, found their way onto the pelmet above the window. The resultant silhouettes created on the mottled mosaic of the floor used to keep him occupied for hours on end. His youthful restlessness found some peace in deciphering some meaning from the "solar' drawings on the floor.

He recalled with fondness the day Archana had entered his life. A petite young thing, on an exchange program for students from Kerala, she had lost her way and was asking him the way to the canteen. He had been busy studying the length of the shadow of the electric pole on the playground and idly calculating its height. Before her query reached his preoccupied mind, the intrusion of a flying dupatta reflected in close conformity to his picture jerked him out of his reverie. She had been irritated at having to ask him a third time, when he offered to take her there.

This chance meeting had set them off on an exciting voyage of discovery about each other. He learned about her interest in pottery and village handicrafts. She was diffidently allowed entry into his private world of transcendental art. Pictures seemed to have a mind of their own, revealing themselves when the Sun chose to do so and revealing a new facet everyday; sometimes every minute too. The sheer filigree work the Sun created on their walls and floor space intrigued and beguiled. Lace shadows with the Sun as the divine artist. Life took on new meanings and new colours.

When the natural culmination of this union had resulted in the birth of a bouncy baby boy, their whole world had changed, filled with colours and music and joy. He had known intuitively that his son would share in his parents' love for the sun-dappled pictures. There was a new dimension to this as they would excite his interest by playing the reflected light from their wrist watches on to the wall, and see him jump up and down trying to catch the moving lights.

Awakening slowly into such a soul-satisfying ceremony of remembrances was his only solace now. It helped him pass a day of rigorous activity as prescribed for guests of the government like him. The long wail of the siren advancing notice of time out for breakfast jolted him into movement as he rushed through his morning's ablutions and raced to join the queue for breakfast and prison duty. It would be three months more before he could go back home after serving time for drunken driving that had taken the life of a footpath sleeper in the small hours of the morning.

# The Registrar's Office

She sat still on the red plastic chair that had served its life sentence there, seemingly in the service of the common man. It appeared as much on its last legs as she did. The yarn in her hand had been knotted before and she had saved it from becoming a kitchen rag by painstakingly unravelling it and rolling it again on a broken twig that she had picked up from the garden adjoining the office. Neem trees dotted the roadside, offering shade to a lot of loiterers. They waited for their roles in the sordid life stories of others. They were unofficial witnesses to anything that a registrar's office needed, be it births, deaths, marriages, divorces or even sales. They were hangers on of a different calibre. They stood about the registrar's office, smoking and drinking innumerable cups of tea and waiting to be called as witnesses. This they did with zeal as each signature got them one more meal.

Parvati was not exactly in need of a job. Nor was she in need of a meal. She was busy doing some sleuthing of her own. She was sure she had seen what she had seen in the same compound as the office. She knew too that those people would return. The oldest of them had fought a lot with the others in the group. "I would not be surprised if they do him in," she thought cheerfully. She had taken time off from her present job as a salesperson to be where she was.

It was only a matter of time, she told herself. She could wait. She proceeded to spend time as fruitfully as she could under the circumstances by reading a bit, or by assiduously knitting a set of woollen sweaters for her young nephew in Bhopal. Lost in pleasant memories of a wriggling bundle of joy two years ago, she almost did not see the arrival of a huge sports utility vehicle that drew to a halt in front of her. She literally jumped out of her skin as she realized that what she had been waiting for had really happened, leaving her gaping stupidly at the occupants.

They jumped out one by one, all five of them. The elder, obviously the father, had a very sombre look. It was evident by the stiffness of his back that he had decided in favour of the others in his family and did not like it even one bit. The others too were less jubilant, probably not wanting to hurt the old man's sentiments. Anyway, there they were, waiting and watching and murmuring amongst themselves. The tea vendor brought his wares at the right time, drawing the group away and allowing Parvati the freedom to sidle up to the car.

She peeked into the back seat and was highly pleased to see that the upholstery was a perfect maroon in satin. The knobs holding the window panes in position were polished a deep burnished copper. The stays on the letdown door at the back did not let her down. They were covered in the same black heavy duty rubber that she had known would be there. How it should make a difference to her was a matter of conjecture. She ran her hands fondly over its smooth green curves. Hers was a sensually satisfying, mood-uplifting caress that bespoke her interest in the vehicle. She looked earnestly at the tiny slot under the wheel, willing herself to be able to read the mileage done. She slowly opened the door and slid into the driver's seat and closed her eyes.

She was in a dream world all her own. "Aah! To own this vehicle," she thought. A 1961 model Willy's Jeep that she had loved and enjoyed and thought she would never have separated from. Her mother had been forced to sell it after her dad died. She remembered how much she had fought over the sale. In the end, she had given way after threatening to fast until it was brought back. But economics took precedence over sentiment and life rolled on. She had taken up a job with a popular second hand car sales company as their star sales person. This she knew would put her in place if ever the jeep came on the market. She came out of her reverie to see the old man nod understandingly at her absorption with the feel of the car. He opened the door and helped her down and drove his baby away with a smiling wave of his hand.

Deeply satisfied, Parvati stepped back into her real world; she had wanted to do this ever since she had seen the vehicle in the neighbourhood three months ago.

# The Tiara

The diamonds scintillated in the evening light. All eighteen of them shone, twinkled, glistened, and lured even the most disinterested window shopper. Neeraja was not disinterested. Instead, she was extremely interested. She had been planning on buying just such a tiara ever since she had seen it on Jenny's head. She made her wish known to her family at the dining table. That was when all hell broke loose.

Her brothers scoffed at her. "You? You can't wear it for your wedding. First find someone who will marry you. Then ask approval for your fancy headgear," they said, laughing at her. Her fond father only shrugged helplessly at the antics of his misguided daughter and her insensitive siblings. Her mother silently promised Lord Ganesha another twelve coconuts if he saved her daughter from her silly fancies.

She remembered Neeraja the day of her best friend Jenny's wedding. Jenny looked ethereal and fairy-like in her beautiful white frilled dress, with a long train behind her. The tiara on her head had created quite a stir, the guests gushing over her radiant beauty as much as over the shining trinket on her shampooed head. Neeraja could not stop sighing over it. She kept trying it on her own head, much to her friends' amusement. Nothing daunted, she decided she would wear such a piece on her wedding day too.

Time passed and the incident was forgotten until she made her latest announcement. The people sitting round the table looked at her aghast. Now what caused her to talk about buying a tiara? "What happened now?" their eyes seemed to ask. She looked shyly down and said simply, "I have found the person of my choice."

Her father's jaw fell in sheer disappointment. Her mother looked thunderstruck. "Hey Ganesha," she prayed. "Where are you now?" She wrung her hands in desperation. Her sole support in these instances, her doctor father was no more. Her husband, she knew, was no help at all. He became nervous if asked to make decisions where his daughter was concerned.

Very quietly, she tousled her darling daughter's head. In a voice full of pain-mingled love, she asked her who she had chosen to be her spouse. Neeraja pointed out of the open door where a man and his "seeing" dog stood. "Mamma, he is blind from birth. He cannot see my burnt face and broken teeth. We have been friends for some time. He is tired of being lonely and so am I. Will you not say yes?" she pleaded.

# An Honest Day's Work

The straps were harsh. They were tight and cut into the skin such that every night his sons had to rub his swollen limbs back to life. They used unguents and ointments of exotic name and fame. He however knew that his time had come. Soon, he would have to give up. He would have to resign himself to the morbid boredom of growing old. He had had a good run and life had been more than fair to him. His beautiful wife had borne him two sons, who, by the grace of God, were intelligent and smart.

The two boys, like their mother before them, had taken to his way of life without any complaints or questions. The younger one, in fact, would come up with interesting solutions to his logistic problems. It was he who had bought the new nylon straps that he lately used. He had found for him the right kind of makeup that would wash off without a trace whenever he needed to appear in polite society. To carry off this facade for so long without detection was not an easy joke. He chuckled to himself at the times when his cover had very nearly blown off. Yes, he nodded to himself. Between God and his two sons, he had had a good run.

This was his last day. The sweet young woman, no old; she seemed young because of an underlying sense of naiveté, seemed to be on a trip after a long time. He watched the gay abandon with which she sang songs off key in competition with her young adult children. The girl was savvy. That he sensed from the way she hovered over the vendors, not letting even one come near her vulnerable mother. The son seemed to be in a dream world of his own. He seemed to be busy with his cell phone all the time. Girlfriend, he presumed.

He loved the way the mother's eyes shone at the sight of the beads in the young gypsy's hands. She favoured the vibrant colours of purple, ochre yellow and crimson red. She must have been a very passionate wife he thought to himself. Suddenly he realized he was thinking of her as a widow. Now, why was that? It was not so obvious. As he watched, he realized the protective air of her two children and her own lost and forlorn look when she was quiet. Will my wife mourn for me this way? Suddenly uncomfortable with his own musings, he jerked into action.

He hoisted the schoolbag with its collection of key chains, nail cutters, shining glass paper weights, earrings, and such like trinkets on to his shoulders with practiced ease. Hanging the round hanger full of similar stuff around his neck such that each one could be viewed without much handling, he propelled his skateboard forward. It was fitted with the big-sized castor wheels that his son had got for him from the second-hand market.

Nearing the woman and her family, he peddled his wares with a great show of bravado; he did not want anyone's pity, his stance seemed to say. Just buy these things from me and let me make my honest way in this world. He saw the turmoil in the young woman's eyes as she made her choices. She did not want to show her pity at his plight. He however knew she empathized with him and his disability. She looked at the stumps of his legs and looked away at once. She was embarrassed at her own curiosity. She was dying to know how he had lost his legs. Her tell-tale emotions were evident on her fluid face and in the five hundred rupee note she handed to him. She refused to take the change. "Keep it," she said.

His last day at work had been more than fruitful. He shrugged to himself at the kindness of the human race as he made his way home with his sons walking behind at a discreet distance. They looked after his needs when he was hungry, or when he needed someone to look out for the burly railway police patrolling the long distance trains. From tomorrow he would be walking straight. He would become the common man on the road.

# The Swansong

They said she sang well. Quite a few of the regulars who jostled for seats or standing room in the crowded locals vouched that she had a great voice. She had an unnamed fan club going, with some knowledgeable travellers even asking her to sing a few songs of their choice. The more vociferous of her critics would self consciously lower their voices when she started to strum her single stringed instrument.

That day was no different when she took her place near the door of the moving train. She sang on and on. Her voice rose to stray heights and sunk to lonely depths. After all, this was her song. This was the song of her life that only she knew how to sing. She did not have to adhere to any of the rhythms that she had been coached in nor keep time to all those assiduously learned beats.

She plucked slowly at the tightly wound strings on her memory scale, pacing her voice to the emotions her thoughts raised. The unconditional love of a parental caress rose to the painful crescendo of an obsessive protection and careened unguarded on the pinnacle of a tortured separation. Slowly and surely her voice faded into a shadow of mangled feelings remembering the bittersweet joys of a reunion triggered by the birth of her daughter.

How well her joys found space in the dulcet tones mesmerizing the passersby. Those who stopped to listen realized the mix of joy and sorrow, coloured with silvery hope clothing the darkest of fears. Plaintive tears mingled with the murmur of satiated desires, incomplete dreams stroked achieved goals. This was her best rendition. None she had known in life was there to admire her music. A divine glory etched its message of purity on her ringing tones. Listeners held their breath as she slowly let out her last ones, and then she was no more.

# *Exhibition*

Her family looked on in shocked disbelief. What was the meaning of it all? Dada, Baba, Ma, and Puchki carefully schooled their faces into a similar frieze- one of cautious query. Each exhibited a slight inclination to applaud provided the answers were more laudable than the presentation.

Baba looked slowly around. He inched closer to Ma. "Is it that I am aging?" he wheezed. Each one looks so raw and unfinished. I am not sure I really approve of my granddaughter's notions of art. "Impossible! This is not the way we brought her up. Tchchah!" With a definite shake of his snow white head, Baba quietly slipped into a corner seat and pretended to be unknown to the artist whose works were on display at the prestigious Fine Arts Gallery in Mumbai.

Ma shepherded her younger one in front of her. Her sharp eyes had noticed a reporter edging their way. Promptly she pushed through the thronging crowd to the information counter and asked for a brochure. "I hope that at least this will throw some light on what your sister is doing here." she said. She flinched in uncontrollable distaste on seeing the pictures of the sculptures on the brochure. She found a seat nearby where she could rest her tired feet and proceed with her reading.

Dada seemed less tense than the others. He was quietly watching the visitors and gauging their reactions. He was at the same time seriously studying those of the exhibits that got the maximum responses and drawing his own inferences. He looked up to see his mother's disturbed glance seeking him out. "Thank God your father is not here today," she mouthed at him silently.

"See the obscene forms. They are all half naked. Some are so incomplete. Eesh! Just look at that one there. That woman seems so wanton. Why did Sheela make an arm stretch out of that pot? Like a beggar? That arm is so long. The pot is ugly. It looks like blood stains seeping out of it. What is all this? Oh! I cannot bear the shame. What will people say?" And she slowly sat herself down once again in abject despair.

The next day being a Sunday, there were three different newspapers and their supplements delivered early in the morning. The whole family fought to see the reviews and the previews, the critics and their comments and read the comments of the arty crowd that had been present in the auditorium. There was a hush in the house as Baba read aloud from his paper.

Sheela is the city's latest find and pride. Her works of art exhibited in the Mumbai Art Gallery for the last three days was a runaway success. She spent three months with the people of Bhopal. She studied their condition after the Gas tragedy that took away so much of their lives. The resultant work of art has placed her in the country's top bracket of artists. Such a sensitive response to the plight of thousands of people who had been living through hell has never been seen before. Each and every sculpture here is an artist's ode to the gutsy survivors of the Bhopal Gas tragedy...A small tear rolled down the old man's cheeks as he murmured, "My granddaughter is a grand granddaughter."

# The Fence

Their three houses had a common fence. Rather, it was a fence that ran the full length of one house and cut perpendicular to the long side separating the smaller two houses. It was well maintained and reflected the quite elite homes it cordoned. Rita and Lisa were the smaller owners and Ksini the owner of the bigger homestead. The three of them would team up at the corner where the fence met the long side and have a heart to heart chat. They met regularly. They had tiny makeshift seats to sit on while talking, on their side of the walls, and life went on smoothly, until...

Ksini being the more prosperous of the threesome and for who the meeting point formed part of the longer compound wall enjoyed some comforts. Her seat was marble, and was reached by a set of beautiful marble steps cut into the wall. Pots of ferns and small flowering plants with their sweet scent made the daily gossip session much more enjoyable. Flasks of tea and trays of freshly made butter biscuits complemented the trade-off of juicy information about their neighbours. Every event in their area and some from the not so close ones were discussed threadbare.

Seated under the genteel canopy that protected their fair complexions they commented upon those of the populace that crossed their path. Their frequent tete-a-tetes served to keep them ahead of the newsmongers, even ahead of the uncouth village gossip, an ungainly hag. They were able to laud one another, give comfort or offer succour as the occasion demanded. They also learned from each other's experiences. In short, they were the best of friends.

Rita and Lisa shared the same birth year and month and were just a few days apart in age. They were, however, as alike as could be imagined. Rita was thin and spare with charming public school manners. She thrived on spicy and junk food, as much as Lisa loathed them. While the former was slim in spite of her intake, the latter was so because of her Spartan tastes. A dietaholic to the core, she espoused every new ruse to get thinner, including long walks in the deep dark woods and surviving on protein drinks.

Ksini was a different kettle of fish altogether. Her regal bearing and arrogant airs belied a loving nature that cared deeply for those who she knew. She could not bear atrocities of any kind more so if it was imposed on women. With her buddies, however, she was very different. Naughty days had them chortling over brandy-filled chocolates and bawdy jokes about their kith and kin.

Thus it was that one eventful day found the three friends in a close huddle. Lisa was in tears. "How could anyone do this to him?" she spluttered. She was in agony over her cousin's plight. He had been terrifyingly Bobbitted and found bleeding profusely on the road outside his house. His pleas for mercy had fallen on deaf ears. Lisa was recounting the happenings at the village square. She reminded them of the other two similar instances that had happened in the last year. Her two friends looked on in unease and distress. Each had ample reason to know that the man was indeed in need of discipline. They however knew that they could not increase their friend's agony with the truth.

Ksini had been showing signs of withdrawal, the days following the shocking event. Rita's looks darted queries at her. Lisa also seemed to be thinking a lot. The meetings of the threesome were getting to be sombre affairs now. When Rita observed that the two of them seemed to be sparring each other in a covert way, they brushed off the allegations and made conscious efforts to revive the bonhomie they always shared.

The morning's newspapers had it in double thick black headlines. *Kunjalakesini, a remarkable woman entrepreneur, commits suicide. Lisa and Rita rushed over to their fence and looked aghast at the police in the neighbouring house. In great agitation and fluster, they sought answers that they knew would be unconvincing. She was not a person of such weakness or cowardice.*

They found a note in her jewel box. "Sorry my friends, He was the last of the three who destroyed my youth. I had to avenge my treatment at his hands. Unfortunately fate decreed that he be Lisa's brother. I cannot see the sorrow on Lisa's face. I bid you goodbye "was the terse message contained within.

# Long, Long Ago

The text message was puzzling in the extreme. It said, "Did Kantan from long, long ago call you?" Dilip had read the message and drawn her attention to it. There was an air of disquiet in his eyes as he told her about it. The worst part of it was that she really could not remember anyone called Kantan.

Coming on top of their recent spat over his chic and fashionable secretary flirting with him at the office year end party, this message was a disaster. She could not think of an adequately acceptable answer to his unspoken queries. She remembered her own vociferous protests; her resounding slap when he objected to her tone of voice, and she flinched. For God's sake, who was this Kantan from long, long ago?

There was not much she could do but wait. Her frantic calls to the sender of the message were being left unattended. She had no explanation to offer, and sought refuge in the mundane regimen of a fastidious homemaker. Her work suffered, however, as she could not concentrate, and managed to spill the smelly disinfectant twice on the hall carpet.

Dilip was biding his time, doing his chores in slow motion, seemingly in no hurry to leave for the office. He cast disparaging looks at her and the cell phone on its stand. He seemed to be castigating her for whatever the message seemed to imply. Is it right that you should have someone from long ago call you so soon? Hell, the effects of the party and its aftermath had not cooled down yet. The hall in the clock had cuckooed its eight chime routine. There was however no sign of Dilip leaving for office.

In her anxiety and tension, she seemed to be stuttering and stammering. This only caused Dilip's urbane eyebrows to rise higher and higher in quizzical mien. She cursed her memory for failing in her hour of need and causing so much heartburn. There must be a sane solution to this mystery, she was sure. Just who could it be? She had had only one really serious fling and Dilip was very much aware of that episode in her life. Woefully aware of the complications this person from her past could bring into her relationship with her husband, she sat down to pray.

The Ping of the cell on the hall table froze the very air in the room. She did not move from her place, mentally willing Dilip to check the message and hoping it was an answer to her prayers. The message read, "Kantan is a dear friend, who has started an online library called www.longlongago. in. Please do take a membership," read Dilip, in increasingly relieved tones, as he settled down to a hearty breakfast of burnt toast and runny cereal.

# The Connoisseur

He loved the new fashions that women subscribed to these days. Their conscious efforts to glamorize mundane existence with flashes of colour always served to inspire him to higher levels of creativity. The newest girl on the block where he lived would work some flashy colour into her toilette. One day it was chrome yellow satin ribbons binding her lustrous brown hair, or a bright pink sweater to go with her blue jeans and labourer's dull green smock. She surprised him totally one day by wearing a cap fitted with streamers of various hues.

He took painstaking notes in a book that he carried everywhere with him. He would flick it out when he saw a well-dressed prospect and quietly follow her to wherever she would stop at least for a few minutes. At the first opportunity, he would quickly draw a rough sketch of the object of his interest and then move on in search of other possibilities.

He was a perfectionist. His target women were all well dressed, attractive and carried themselves with confidence. They were invariably as tall as he was, had broad shoulders, and walked well. Sometimes they were dark, sometimes light. At times, they were loud; at others, squeaked like rats. Some were shrill too. Not all that however mattered as long as they dressed well or differently and became the objects of his passionate interest.

Then he set out in search of the material. He had to get the exact textures, the perfect matches, the best accessories to go with all the designs that he produced. Even the undergarments were assiduously matched for colour and style. He had no qualms going up to the assistant at the lingerie department to seek her help to choose the best fit.

At the jewellers, the helpers who were mostly women marvelled at the ease with which he made his choices. He set the clothing out on the table. Oblivious to the admiring oohs and aahs, he chose the exquisite sets that would go best with each ensemble. They would watch in silent jealousy of the woman who was to receive these gifts.

After a frugal meal of bread and soup, which he ate very slowly, he prepared for the evening ahead. He thought sadly of his loveless marriage and of his buxom homely wife and shed a lonely tear. She would not understand his needs or his obsession with women's fashion. She had called him names that questioned his manhood. He was hurt. That did not stop him from his pursuits. He loved his job he told himself with a shake of his head, as he stepped into the basement office where he looked at his silent companions and beamed happily. He set out to dress the mannequins in their finest best before wheeling them into the shop windows.

# The Frozen Shoulder

The frozen shoulder was giving her a lot of trouble. It was apparent to anyone that she was troubled. There was no gainsaying the fact. Part of the reason was that she had never heard of or seen a frozen shoulder ever before in her young life. Coming from the most rural of rural areas, she had absolutely no idea what to do with a frozen shoulder.

She thought of calling home. But it was fairly late in the morning and she knew her mom would be busy shopping in the mall. That was her favourite pastime and hated to be disturbed in her perambulations. She remembered hearing her mother muttering angrily under her breath when once long ago, dad had called her on her cell to tell her of a fire in the neighbourhood of their home. So, she desisted.

Now what could she do? Her nearest neighbour was a real dear. She kept advising her every time she set eyes on her about the ways and means to keep her husband home bound. It was laughable really, but old Mrs. Lobo was of the opinion that all newly married young girls needed to be advised on this issue.

That left the grocer in the corner shop. Praiji was a kind man, but hard of hearing. She could imagine the scene she would create if she had to shout her queries across the counter. Ooh! The scandal! The neighbours would all gather then to give their opinions. Someone might even comment on how badly brought up she was, bringing such a simple issue as a frozen shoulder to the street. She shuddered in distaste and turned her eyes on the bookshelf.

Her husband was a voracious reader. He read almost everything he could lay his hands on. His bookshelf reflected his multi-pronged taste. There were books on law, constitution, Histories of other races and cultures, autobiographies, story books for all ages and cookbooks of every cuisine in the world. That was when she saw it and sighed happily. "At last", she thought as she saw the title of the booklet 'Frozen Shoulders'. She took it out of its place and flipped open the pages in a great hurry. She was very, very disappointed to see a medical discourse on frozen shoulders. It did not answer her question and left her in a greater dilemma than ever before.

Tired and dispirited, she went and sat at the telephone table. What to do? Who to ask? That was when she saw the advertisement in the top corner of the first page of the newspaper. "Ask Me", it declared; for all queries on frozen shoulder". There was a phone number at the bottom of the advertisement. With great hope, she dialled the number. In a voice tremulous with the hope of at last getting her question answered, she said "Please can you tell me how to thaw this frozen pork shoulder that I must cook for my husband's dinner tonight?"

# The Sister

Santhamma loved her traditions. She enjoyed the smell of the water as it hit the dry hard muddy patch at the gate. She sprinkled the water all round, then swept the hard floor with a coconut frond broom. Very diligently she counted out the dots of the design she had planned to lay out that day. With practised ease she dribbled the rice powder through her bent fingers, and sighed in pleasure at the beautiful pattern that gave expression to her creativity.

Satisfied with the fruit of her labour, she re-entered the house locking the main door behind her. Soon enough the sound of a brisk char char char heralded the smell of freshly roasted coffee berries. This personal attention to the best plantation and pea berry seeds, bought from the coffee board outlet in town was another of the mainstays of her routine. The top container of the two part filter had to be dunked in hot water and then held over the flame to dry. She would not dream of using the recycled old blouse to dry the wet vessel.

The strong aroma of homemade filter coffee mingled with the smell of the day's news as Santhamma's husband turned the pages of his paper. His eyes fell on the inert forms of sleeping children on colourful mats on the floor. He was about to remonstrate with his wife for letting them sleep beyond six in the morning, when there was a knock on the door. Santhamma looked up expectantly asking "who's there?" Promptly came the reply, "Lakshmiamma, Lakshmi". Hearing this, the happy mother woke her children saying; "see, Lakshmi is knocking on the door. Welcome Lakshmi (the goddess of wealth) into the house" Obediently the door was opened to let in the servant who by virtue of her auspicious name was invaluable to her mistress's scheme of things.

The day of Diwali dawned. More than any other day, this one was very important. Santhamma had repeatedly told her servant to come in early on D-Day. Promptly at five a knock sounded and as usual was received with the well rehearsed "Who's there?" routine. The answer came loud and clear "Lakshmi's sister, amma, Lakshmi's sister"

All hell broke loose at this answer, as Santhamma in a fit of rage almost beat the sister for coming and announcing herself in that manner. Her Diwali was ruined as instead of the usual answer of Lakshmi, she had been told "Lakshmi's sister". She explained to a much traumatized husband, that Goddess Lakshmi's sister was none other than MooDevi the harbinger of poverty and penury. "Just imagine that stupid girl went on a holiday and sent her sister to us on such an auspicious day "and she wailed loudly. Without Lakshmi at the door, her Diwali was now spoiled.

# A Fear-y Tale

The sun shone through the green canopy above, dappling the forest path that she trod daintily and carefully. She had always been warned of the dangers of walking alone in the forests. No lurking threat could however stop her from traipsing along the various paths that she knew so well and loved even more.

She looked into all the secret nooks and crannies of the nesting birds checked on a huge spider whose one meter wide web fascinated her. There were the remnants of two big dragon flies and a few yellow crushed butterfly wings. Shuddering a bit, she moved back on to the path and went her adventurous way. She had a whistle in her pocket which would bring help to her in a jiffy, and she knew that well.

She climbed the tiny hillock, where behind the thorny bushes at the top she had seen a bird's nest. Built into the thickest portion of the underbrush, the little architectural wonder protected nature's most vulnerable babies. Parting the bushes carefully, she drank in the sight of the nestlings "cheep cheeping" away, with one worried parent weighing the odds. He viewed her intrusion with distrust and suspicion and made ready for battle.

Two more sojourns vied for attention before she reached her destination. Lady Rabbit lived in the foliage just behind the berry patch. She had stumbled upon it by chance one day while looking for wild flowers to give her mom. She had startled the poor thing into revealing her precious home and like all creatures of the wild, she too had held its secret and not told anyone about it. Ever since, her visits to this part of the world would include a peek into the burrow.

A slight chillness hurried her toward the ancient well with its lone tortoise. The well had a spring in it which kept the well in water through the year. There were channels cut in the ground into which the water was run so that the forest animals could drink their fill. The wolves too came here. When the well was full the water ran into the troughs. In summer however, when the levels were low, a hand pump was used to bring silvery relief to the thirsty.

Espying the old thatch roofed cottage hiding under the clinging green ivy and other coloured creepers, she stopped. A spark of mischief shone in her beautiful blue eyes as she ran to the huge brass knocker, banged it once and ran and hid behind the big wooden flower pot holding fragrant yellow marigolds. The door opened to reveal a massive figure, swathed in night-clothes and lace cap and wearing an enormous pair of pink rimmed spectacles on its huge, bulbous nose.

Seeing no one at the door, the figure banged the door shut and stomped away. Convulsed with laughter at her little ploy to trouble grandma, she almost stood up to repeat her ruse.

She stopped. Something was wrong. That was not grandma at all. She sat back behind the huge pot and thought it out.

In a short while she went round the cottage and peeked in through the curtained windows. There! She saw it again. This time she was very sure that something was very wrong. Repairing back into the green glades, she took her whistle out, unscrewed it and flattened it out into a small cell phone. She sent out a message of SOS and settled down to wait.

In less than five minutes she could hear the whir of blades in the sky and before she could say Little Red Riding Hood, there was her father with his trusty laser gun. Dad, that animal there is a wolf. I saw its hairy legs under the night shirt. His feet are too enormous to fit into her shoes. How foolish that anyone thought I would fall for the same trick, no papa? Please save grand mama.

Little Red's dad did the needful and flew away in the snazzy helicopter that the royalties from his first book "Little Red Riding Hood" had enabled him to buy.

# The Last Bow

It was in the air. One could feel it. The end was nigh. One could hear it in the slipping timbres of the voices. In the finality of papers being folded and folded again. In the sharp crease caused by every fold; in the tear that wet the final crease. It could be seen in the slope of the shoulders. Once Amazonian in build now slipped into shadows, the unwavering gazes were watery graves of long surrendered dreams. The bouncy strides had become wimp like slouches shunting from one supportive wall to the other.

Meghan found it difficult to focus on the work at hand. Could it be that the lens had got scratched from bad handling? She knew she had been careful; especially as she had borrowed the pair from the old lady in the park, just for this occasion. Anyway, she shrugged. Who really cares? No one would see her handiwork. Each would be busy with what he or she had to say. Everyone would come, make their presences felt and go back to whatever unfinished business they had left behind.

Gingerly she picked up the glass of water at her bedside. She peered into it, probably looking for mosquitoes or some such light insects. Flicking her unpinned hair from her eyes, she bent to take a sip and stopped. Her wrinkled hands shivering a little, she saw Ruth almost rise from her seat to take the tumbler from her hands. She shook a peremptory finger at her, warning her from showing up her weakened state. Meghan was enjoying this moment of truth. She showed her glee at their discomfort. Ruth, her husband, and their son Neal looked self-consciously caring. Her own family having passed on a few years earlier, she had been forced to seek the attentions of her sister Ruth and her family.

Now the time had come for her to move to the senior care centre downtown. She was required to make a will in favour of her sister or nearest relative and sign the admission forms for the centre. Cackling to herself, Meghan lifted the papers and handed it to her sister who promptly dropped it, in sheer clumsiness. What followed was a bit of an anti climax, with Meg pouring the water over the papers and bursting into loud and uncontrolled laughter. She went into a spasm of coughing from which she never gained consciousness. The curtain came down on the tableau of a family on the verge of getting a huge endowment. The looks of horror on their faces and that of disappointment on the maid's, and the contorted figure on the bed was what stayed with the highly appreciative audience as they made their way out of the auditorium.

# To Life

The train was running late. Having had breakfast earlier on, I was on the lookout for something different to ease the monotony of the railway menu. The Coromandel, moved slowly into Rajahmundry station, and drew to a stop. No sooner had I espied the Fresh Juice stall than I jumped out and ran to get my favourite grape juice. I had paid and taken the token for the drink when I saw the train begin to move.

Oh my god, I was about to lose my train and my bag was in the compartment with all the jewels I had planned to wear at my nephew's wedding. Panic set in, and I raced to the nearest set of steps which would get me to my coach. Unfortunately, many others like me had been caught unawares, and were running to the same set of steps as I. Getting a foothold on the lowest step, I reached for the shining guard rail to hold and climb into the carriage.

Till today I do not know how, but my hand clutched at nothing and I felt myself falling one way then another. In slow motion, I saw myself slipping into the gap between the running train and the platform, and heading towards imminent death. Suddenly a hand shot out from nowhere and held me by my right hand which I had been flailing, seeking a hold. Soon three more hands held on and I found myself suspended, over the platform with the train slowly picking up speed. I was dangling waist down over the edge of the platform. The jutting steps of each coach that crossed behind me, banged into the back of my thighs, Thoughts of my vulnerable little children back home, one preparing for her tenth exams and the other a mischievous imp, raced into my mind and I prayed for a miracle.

All the while, the bang bang bang was going on. I could hear shouts, and pandemonium in the hazy background. As suddenly as the trauma started, it ceased. Someone had pulled the chain to stop the train. I was dragged back to the platform, where I stood in shivering shame, when a dirty old tattered shawl was thrown around me. I remembered the old beggarly individual sitting on one of the stone seats, who I had passed, on my way to the snacks shop. I had registered his presence with a shudder, and a distasteful look thinking him dirty and beggarly.

Someone fetched my by now torn sari that had caught on one of the moving steps and parted ways with me in my hour of need. I was being asked if I wanted to disembark and be admitted to hospital, and much more. Wrapping my own silks around me and vigorously refusing all need to be hospitalized, I sought the old man who had saved my life and my dignity

He was nowhere near the train. I could not return his shawl, nor thank him. For a long time after, I worried if he had seen my shudder at his dirty state and so refused my pretensions to civility? I only know I felt ashamed of myself then and still do when I think of that day. I had learned my lesson however, and always stop to think before passing judgment on people or situations around me. Today, I hold my tongue. I know I am a better person, because of that one act of a strange old man in an unknown setting, where I had made a rash and erroneous assumption, and lived to grieve my arrogance. Thank you, kind old man, wherever you are.

# Ouija Board

This happened many moons ago when I was in the first year of my Undergraduate Course. It was an all women's college. It was also the season for mad hatters, I think. Inclement weather kept us indoors in class, and raring for mischief. We had raided the room meant for students' lunch boxes earlier, and gorged ourselves on all things food and fine! Talk shifted to things occult and one among the group began a discussion on the Ouija board. A general consensus got the girls talking highly of the board as a trusty means of connecting with the dear departed.

Soon, a make-shift board was brought in- a fairly big piece of cardboard, covered with black chart paper and the alphabets and numbers chalked out on it. We started our calls to the nether world, and those of us present who had lost relatives within the last two months started their "calls" Needless to say, some of us believed, some did not, and some were fence- sitters, ready to boo or bawl, according to the need.

I took charge of the neat white chalk, doing the rounds, when the volume of boos increased in strength (the booers objected to the spelling mistakes, and said even ghosts have a spelling sense) Thus started my misadventure. I called upon my recently demised grandfather, and my hand of its own volition traced out his name and age on the board, in reply to my query of proof of the spirit being my relation.

The first question he answered was of course about what ranking each present would get in the university exams. Everyone was truly surprised to note that grandfather was able to pinpoint each person by name! Oops! The next question pertaining to boyfriends was answered with vague references to fat girl on the right and the one in blue and all that. This got the non believers giggling and the believers upset.

I was kneeling down, over the board on the ground, so I was able to see out from under the door. Some sari covered feet were approaching our closed door from a few feet away. So I asked grandpa to please come into the room and talk with us. Just then there was a knock on the door and everyone froze!!! None would open the door from a fear of having to face a spirit outside. The knock got repeated, and my friend and I just doubled up in laughter. Before we could check ourselves and get up to open the door, the door was literally banged open and there stood an apparition I least expected to see...our principal!

She naturally did not join in the 'spirit' of the scene, and dragged two dispirited souls to her chamber! We escaped suspension, but my fingers still ache when I think of the imposition I wrote!

ALL MY OFFERINGS MAY PLEASE BE TAKEN WITH A PINCH OF SALT!

# The Diary

Sweetie entered her room and stopped short. There was an intangible sense of intrusion. The faint scent of yesterday's perfume which would have normally greeted her nostrils was not there. Nor was the heavy atmosphere of a room kept closed for two days. She pushed the door inward and peered inside, an intruder in her own private space.

Following the ray of sunlight she traced it to the source- an open window on the far wall. The curtains had been slightly moved, allowing the intruder to see. Even the contents of her dressing table had been moved around in a furtive endeavour. Furtive! She decided. Someone had rummaged the contents of the drawer, she was sure. It was slightly open, almost as if it was meant to be opened again.

The curtain moved a bit and she saw her mother, leaning into the sunlight, squinting at a book. Her Diary! Sweetie was aghast! How could she? How dared she? She fumed inwardly, knowing well enough that she would never accost her adoptive mother with the sneaky act. Quietly she moved back to the main house and, sitting in the darkened drawing room, mulled over what she had seen, and how to tackle it. Hearing the quiet swish of her door closing, she sat up wanting to scream and curse.

Highly incensed and wanting to fight, she announced her presence by getting up and stretching herself and announcing that her bus had come in early. "What's for lunch?" she queried, mentally planning how and when to tackle her. Her mother showed her pleasure at her presence and hugging her said, you get whatever you order. "Such feigned innocence!" thought Sweetie angrily and reeled out a list of highly improbable items.

As she prepared to go into her room, her mom called out. Just a minute, dear, I'm off to the mall Papa will be waiting for me. Have your breakfast, and don't wait lunch for us." Saying which she moved out before Sweetie could say anything.

In a tizzy from the activities of the past hour, Sweetie went into her room and took out her diary. The page opened at the last entry. Her sneaky parent had made an entry in it Taking a deep breath, she read, "Dearest child, be happy, for your wish is to be granted. Your natural parents are coming today. Don't blame them for leaving you with us. Falsely implicated in a criminal case they have had to undergo a lot of hardship to clear their name. As your parents did not want you to grow up under a cloud, they entrusted you to our care. Papa and I have no hard feelings about your tantrums and your violent reaction when you first knew. We understand. God bless."

# The Trip

The heat was unbearable. So was the tension building inside her. Flexing her fingers and toes, she sat in the bus willing it to move faster. The driver did not seem to be in any hurry. He stopped for every would-be passenger on the road, tossing ribald remarks at all and sundry. His behaviour was getting on her nerves, but she had no option but to sit quietly and pray that he would at least drop her at her destination on time..

What is it in a person that stops him from asking for forgiveness? Prakash could easily have said sorry and the whole thing would have blown over in a minute. They would have gone their different ways as usual. Another meeting would have passed in civilized inaction. Each of them would have taken pride in his or her self control and would have inexplicably prepared for the next get-together in sanguine anticipation of another non event. As a family, they hated confrontation. What a paradox it was. The whole group dreaded meeting but meet they would, at the appointed time, at the appointed place, without a single absentee, without quailing at the expense of money or time!

They just had to open up and talk to Prakash. He was a kind soul. He would listen. He would do as they said. He would say whatever they told him. However, when the time came, none would talk. She was getting tired of the farce. She decided she would break their silence today at any cost.

She would prompt him. "How do you ask for forgiveness? What would you say? SAY IT" That's not cheating. Prompting is not cheating. She would lay emphasis on the central theme and insist that he SAY it.

In the evening when the group had gathered, she put action to her thoughts. Startled, Prakash said "Sorry?" in a loud voice, unaware that his voice had carried. There was a big clapping of backs and everyone congratulated him on getting the word right. Crossword freaks, they were. The family got together to solve the monthly crossword sweepstakes, which was rather tough. This time they vowed that Prakash the youngest sibling barely thirteen should contribute and so they left him just one word to work out...

"Sorry, sorry "Sarla trilled as she jumped out of her seat and promptly fell as the bus screeched to a sudden halt at the traffic lights. She had been dreaming!!

# A Perfect Professional

"That was that". He had made all the arrangements and would have to wait to know the outcome. This was the worst part of the whole exercise. He hated it, but it came with the job. Patience was the first prerequisite. It would prove his worth or lack.

Chiranjeevi was an expert on bombs. His opinions were often sought by people both in the trade and in government. His judgment was trusted without exception. He revelled in his expertise, seeking to establish his superior knowledge by delivering more than promised, every time he was called. Service was his motto, perfection, his creed.

While he waited, he reflected on how well his life was shaping up. Both his kids were in college, His parents were well looked after by his understanding wife, and they reciprocated in kind. Life was smooth like a perfectly set bomb. His dad disliked hearing this metaphor. "Too violent", he was wont to say. For Chiranjeevi however, his vocabulary had been developed around his workplace, and he knew no other. He would usually shrug away these comments.

*His wife was quite annoyed with him for spoiling her plans for a picnic, by claiming an important job that had cropped up.*

*Expressing their displeasure however did not stop them from going ahead with their plans. The children needed to go out somewhere, anywhere. He could surprise them later, if he had the time, he thought.*

"Ten minutes to go". His sharp gaze tried to read the signs at the mouth of the tunnel under the escarpment. The bombs were placed at two meter intervals, and the soft whirring of the timer set in motion reached his ears. Nodding to himself, he looked up at the road on the bridge over the river and had the shock of his life.

His parents were being gently encouraged to climb down the bridge to a seat under a huge banyan tree that was barely two hundred meters from the bomb site. Two minutes to go and he saw his wife gesticulating back at the bridge. With his heart in his mouth, he saw his dawdling youngsters walking oh so slowly. There was nothing he could do from the distance that he was at, but to watch his perfect professionalism destroy his life forever.

# The Journey

The road was long and dusty. It was seven days long, a hungry road, sad and weather beaten, pockmarked with heavy ruts where tired wheels had done valiant duty. A long line of refugees, tired and bedraggled were being pushed and prodded. They were not allowed to rest until the next camp was reached.

Nagamma, her ailing husband and their five children made slow headway. The man was weak, and sick. Tuberculosis had no easy cure, was highly dreaded and feared. This journey however had to be taken. A pall of doom enveloped their camping space, when they reached there. It fell to her second born, Sita's lot to go in search of rations for the children in the morning. Her elder, Ramulu had been forcibly conscripted, and not been heard of since. "Come back soon my dear the soldiers will not let us wait for you if you are late", she warned.

Sita flit between the tents quickly, collected the food packs and raced back on nimble feet. She could sense a presence behind her, and she was scared. Not that she felt intimidated. At the same time, Shakkumma had described some gory incidents in the last camp. Now, she was mortally afraid. Trying to shake off the shadow, lest it followed her to their tent, Sita slipped in and out of the lanes between the rows of shelters, managing at last to reach the sanctuary of her mother's arms.

When the long procession started, Nagamma collected her motley brood, and set off. Their night of rest had helped. The food though sparse was better than nothing. Tying her husband to the plastic chair placed on a rough assemblage of wheels attached to a wooden platform, the family set off. His unceasing cough and spitting caused people to cast pitying looks her way. It did not help that a masked youth prodded them on their way with silent jabs at the rough wheel chair. He did not say much but seemed to look at Sita more often than she could accept without worrying.

The next two days were spent in a daze of trudging hunger, as there was no more bread doled out. Somehow, someone had managed to boil ditch water and brewed tea. Sita managed to procure this milk-less life resource for her family. Her youngest sibling came up with a loaf of day old bread which he said a soldier had thrown at him. Thanking God for small mercies, the meal was partaken of, and the journey resumed.

The closer they seemed to the Indian border, the more they were pushed to move faster. Sita tripped and fell a couple of times. Her thin and emaciated body could take no more. She fainted in a sorry heap. Uttering loud curses and threatening her in typical military style, the masked soldier picked her up and thrust her at her father's feet, on the chair. Nagamma's burden was now bigger, but she carried on. It was another two or three hours more. The sun was setting and soon they would be safe in their own country.

Cries of praise to the deities of their choice rent the air. The sorry picture of suffering humanity entered No Man's land between the two countries. The bickering of their civilized past were re-established. Lines were drawn. Haves and have-nots resumed their scripts. Status Quo had found its place in the safe environs.

Sita found an envelope in the bag hung behind the wheelchair. Wonderingly, she took it out and called her mother. It contained a red bandana, a wad of Indian currency, and a letter. "Amma," it said "I was there with you, throughout the journey. I saw your suffering and could not help. If I dared to show myself, that would have meant sure extinction for all of us. So I took the next best action. I guarded you people so that you would be spared the harassment that you would have otherwise gone through. This money is for you to start your new life. If God wills, I will be with you when the war ends. If not, remember, I never left you. I remain, your dutiful son. Take care. Wave the red cloth near the eastern fence, about ten in the morning. I shall know all is well."

# The Stairs of Fire

There comes in every woman's life, a moment of truth, when she knows better; when she believes in herself, in her mission, and believing, accepts that invisible guiding hand of the Supreme Consciousness. It need not always be a hard fought for moment. It dawns, just dawns, and then like a bright fluorescent ray, prods, directs, guides. She sheds her inhibitions, her social bonds, her self -imposed taboos, and arrives at the threshold of a poignant, pervasive, presentiment. She knows now what lies ahead. What has to be done and how.

Protima had thus arrived-at the moment of truth. She reflected on the awesomeness of the decision taken by her. "Now I have ascended into that select band of people who know what their lives are about," she mused. She got up from her meditative stance, and slowly walked up to the idol at the head of the stairs to the ashram meditation room. Paying obeisance to Lord Ganesh, she thanked Him for his guidance, for making her understand, for empowering her. This self analysis had worked wonders for her morale. Her shoulders were squared, ready to brave the impending future.

Going home was the first and easiest part on her agenda. As indifferent as ever, Atul did not ask about her early return. His mother only cast a cursory glance at her before perching on her regular seat near the balcony railings. Pupul and Putul were too deeply immersed in their Scrabble Board to even notice her. Their collective indifference today was a welcome respite. She needed the time to get used to the new resolve becoming stronger every minute, within her. The tumbling, cascading waterfall of ideas, options, plots and plans, made her quite breathless. She really did not feel like talking to anyone just then.

The next morning dawned bright and sunny. "A good omen" she thought. After all the morning chores, Protima went to her cupboard and started rummaging in her personal files. She was in no haste as her mother in law was out for the day and would not be home for some time. The huge house seemed to engulf her in its repressive silence, even perhaps frowningly discouraging the straggling salesmen on the road from entering. She drafted a letter, wrote and rewrote it to her satisfaction.

Now came the hard part. What should she wear? "Not the pink salwar suit nor the printed sari; nor the magenta and black. It just would not suit the occasion. In the end she settled for a simple black and white starched organdie sari. It made her at once smart and business like. "Thank God, Women's Lib did not burn the sari as well," she smiled to herself. She bound her hair into a tight low, ponytail, and set out to meet the wide wicked world.

The taxi was an extravagance; she felt that it justified the situation. She would have to hurry. The typing pool was close to where she had to go. A wild staccato of noisy, clacking typewriters interspersed with "2 by 1" and "is there any ribbon?" greeted her as she opened the baize door. She selected a middle aged typist who was free, and presented her matter to him. Protima sank down into a vacant seat to wait for her manuscript to be typed. Reaction was setting in. Stupefied by her own show of independence, and her temerity, she heaved a deep sigh and wondered if what she was doing was right or not. She knew however that this was just the beginning. The die was cast. The game had begun, and swim or sink, she knew she would never go back to being her usual retiring self effacing self.

Soon, her work complete, she set off, armed with her manuscript. Her Manuscript, she reminded herself. Stepping briskly into the cool antiseptic interiors of the office complex, she headed for the lift. It was an automatic one the kind which was not manned. Her heart in her mouth, she entered to find that she would have to go up all alone. Terror engulfed her, leaving her quite faint. But even this hurdle was safely crossed when the noiseless machine stopped obediently at the fourth floor to release her. Apprehensive and breathless, she approached the huge plate glass doors in front of her. She could see the busy receptionist talking crisply into a bank of wires and phones on her desk.

Seeming more confident than she actually felt, Protima stepped into the plush air conditioned interior of the successful publisher's office. She had to wait some more, as he had stepped into the news room. A flash of a bright red handkerchief vigorously rubbing a pair of spectacles brought her out of her reverie to gasp at the keen eyes surveying her drooping countenance. Introducing herself, she handed over the papers and sat down even before she was asked.

Mr. Gooptu passed a careless eye over the title, and the first few words. Slowly he sat up straight seeming to take in whole lines at a glance. To Protima, who was preparing to run at the first word of criticism, his increasing interest in the matter he read gave some hope. When however he reached for the bell to summon the peon, she thought "Oh! Oh! Looks like goodbye!" To her great surprise, he asked for some tea, and summoned Mr. Ghosh to the cabin Five minutes passed by when a discreet knock on the door announced a bespectacled avuncular individual to whom the manuscript was given. Mr. Ghosh read through the first few lines and sat up with a start. "Sir," he said, "this will not do at all. Do you know who she is?" "Here it comes", thought Protima and braced herself for the abuses. She saw the publisher's sudden wary stance, and knew now that if she did not talk out, her project was doomed.

"Sir," she began, "let me explain. Yes I am renowned industrialist Atul's wife. That cannot stop me from being creative, can it?" Mr. Gooptu turned to Ghosh for his comment, almost as if he did not want to argue. "Yes, it can. Do you know the effect it will have on the reading public? There will be gossip, and questions; the press will tear you to pieces. What about your family? How about your kids?

Don't you have a responsibility towards them? My God, all the goodwill that Atul sir has built for himself all these years....dust and ashes after the first issue comes out. Are you not ashamed of yourself? Sir, I am absolutely against taking this up". Ghosh turned towards his boss with a frown.

Steep ling his fingers in front of him, Mr. Gooptu proceeded to examine the shape it made in great detail. Noncommittally he asked Ghosh to proceed. Ghosh then argued that lesbianism was taboo and not at all something anyone could write about, so blatantly and so openly. Protima, her arguments ready, pounced on him telling him of the crying need to educate people. "This topic is not taboo. It can never be. We must tell people that this is not an aberration. This is as normal as being heterosexual. It is abnormal to shun discussions. We cannot afford to be like ostriches, with our heads held collectively in the sand. This will save children who try it out for fun and then are stuck in a vicious cycle with no chance of escape. We need to be empathetic in our approach. As a medium of mass communication you have a greater duty to reach researched facts to the ignorant public. What better way, sir? What better way?"

"Just imagine, for those who want an interesting read, the story line is there. Those who are looking for more information, the facts are there. Those who need help can always call me. My contact numbers are there. As to my family's reaction, let me be the judge of that. Okay? From your point of view, your sales will increase. Does that not concern you?" The impish look she cast on Mr. Gooptu was not lost on either of the two men. Ghosh only winced, choosing to keep silent. "Will you react only if you get a call from your own kids? Only if they call and tell you they are in trouble?"

As if on cue, the phone rang which was a welcome distraction from the heat of the argument. A voice distraught with pent up emotion said "Pappa, I am in trouble!" Mr Gooptu's hands flew to the buttons on the phone to shut her voice from the listeners in the room. In a voice quivering with fear he asked "tell me beta, what is it?" "Pappa, Pappa. You will not hate me? Promise if I tell you, you will not hate me?" Hearing the impassioned plea in her voice, Mr. Gooptu's face lost colour, and he slowly sank into his seat. "Tell me my dear, pappa will never hate you," he beseeched. All kinds of scenario chased each other on his face, and left the shocked listeners, speechless. Suddenly the connection was cut. Mr. Gooptu jigged the phone lines trying to make it work. "Oh where did she call from?" He tried her mobile number only to get the busy tone.

Terribly disturbed, the trio waited for the line to ring again which it did, causing Ghosh to jump and take the phone for his boss. "April Fool! Pappa, April Fool" sang a happy voice, and clicked off the connection.

The atmosphere in the room was to be felt to be believed. Mr. Gooptu's obvious relief, washing over him in waves, Ghosh's spluttering, clucking, "Children, these days!" and Protima's 'where do I stand?' looks made for a superb climax scene in a third rate street play. "Ah, Ghosh, I think the moral of the story is that we do not wait for the distress calls from home. Isn't it?" He tried to normalize the charged atmosphere in the room before he asked Ghosh to read through the whole manuscript and then give his report.

Mr. Gooptu formally shook hands with Protima, and commended her for her guts in wanting to talk about such a taboo subject. "Of course I will want to serialize the story" he said, "to get maximum mileage for my magazine, okay? Further I would like you to handle the correspondence that is bound to crop up. That in turn will lead to the creation of an agony aunt column. We will work it out. In appreciation of your guts, I am going to do what no sensible publisher would. I am sanctioning an advance payment for you. Happy?" Her brimming eyes thanked him of their own accord, as she left the room with a polite namaste.

Outside on the kerb, she took a deep breath...of freedom, and breathed out the last of her inhibitions. "The Stairs of Fire", she dramatized. "Wow! Truly the stairs of fire and she had gone up them all alone. Now, she would help other women in similar predicaments. The average Indian Woman needs a prop, and she would be that prop; to thousands of women. She would show them how to handle this kind of a situation. Lesbianism needed to be understood. Not mocked, not ill-treated, and definitely not ridiculed. So God help me," she thought as she hailed a taxi for her return home. Her new life would begin with a crash and a bang as soon as the latest issue of The Tuesday Woman hit the stands and her home.

# Therapist

Four knits followed by four purls, K1P1, K1P1, K1P1... Turn the work. Repeat the same. She followed the instructions line upon line until all the blue wool was over, and then added the pink. The olive green came next followed by the chrome yellow. She went back to school in her mind as she recalled the needlework classes she had missed. She remembered the exam days when all the shirkers in class presented three or four differently coloured pieces to the teacher for marking. It used to be fun. Sometimes they were caught. It was part of the game.

Today she did the same knitting that she had abhorred once. They called it therapy. She hoped to resume all the functions of her hand muscles by knitting lengths of wool. I wonder how long this will take she thought wearily. The doctor had warned her not to be too optimistic. She could barely manage two inches of work in a session. After that, she went home and slept like a log. They would not let her see the child. "Not yet," they said kindly. She imagined the questioning looks in their eyes; the pity; and the judgment. She wrung her heart to shreds before remembering the kind doctor who had assured her that no one knew the case history. No one will know either. He had admonished her to look to the future and build up her energy reserves.

Helen shuddered in horror as the events of that day passed like a movie in her mind. Her job as an assistant to a psychoanalyst had involved taking care of the younger patients in the playroom adjacent to the consulting chamber. This colourfully decorated space had bright balloons running the length of the walls, laughing monkeys and smiling lions cavorting in un-caged freedom looking benignly from the frames of huge posters. The letters of the alphabet seemed to have minds of their own. They frolicked in gay abandon, not bound by any school curriculum. It was here that she had had the worst nightmare of her life.

She had been teaching macramé knots to young Sheila. The little minx had tied the red threads around her wrists and was now topping it with black and white twine. It had started out in fun. Somewhere along the way, she realized that her ward, who was not all there, probably, knew what she was doing when she tied her hands up in knots. She lunged behind the door and took up a cane, which she herself had not known was there. Cane in hand Sheela proceeded methodically to beat her with it. A small sad voice was intoning: "This one is for being good, this one for being rude. This one is for being glad and this one is for turning mad."

The cane cut her face as she tried to catch the brat with her bound hands. The doctor's room opened; seeing him, Sheila jumped up in great glee and wielded the cane at him. Helen stared in horror as instead of stopping her; the doctor encouraged her to beat faster seemingly enjoying the pain. The enormity of the whole scene sank into her as she fell to a faint, dragging an enormous hippo bookshelf on to her hands, which lay crushed under its weight. Her heart went out to the young girl Sheila who had been under the care of that fiend therapist who had made full use of her innocence.

# The Miracle

The shrill cries of children at play, the pleading of matronly ladies with half an ear on the gossip mill, and the other half on the frolicking screeches from the kids wallowing in water at the falls, the gruff laughter of the men at some risqué joke muttered under the breath. Glasses clinked self consciously as cheers sounded.

A couple of family servants had been brought along on the trip, more to serve than to be given a holiday! The scene was idyllic. The families out on a picnic were making sufficient noise to raise the devil. Perhaps they did. There was a sudden swooshing sound of gushing water as if from a spring. Neela heard it first and warned the kids to come up onto higher ground. Sirish undervalued the warning and teasingly told her to pipe down. Yet another yell from the servants told the party they were in trouble. "Sahib, sahib," the older one called frantically. All but one of the kids had been pulled up. The little one Rajeev however was too frightened of the swirling waters. He refused to budge, crying loudly.

Mountain springs tend to swell and subside at will. They had all known that. However they had not prepared for this kind of an eventuality. Jit's wife called out her little one's name coaxing him to climb a wee bit higher, as the watery divide between them and the child widened. The rushing stream was now a raging river bringing with it whole branches, and other such debris. The older children with their servants had climbed sufficiently higher and were temporarily safe. Just then as if out of thin air, could be seen a girl wearing a multi-coloured scarf. She appeared like magic, just behind the baby, and hoisted him up to the waiting servant who eagerly took charge of the screaming infant. The men, who had been climbing to the other side in an effort to reach the kid from above, did not notice her at all.

As fast as the waters had risen it subsided, and the jittery families were united. Pack up time had come in faster than anticipated.

Everyone noticed at the same time that the girl was nowhere to be seen. Explanations were made and re made about how she had come to save the child. The men folk went in search and came back without a clue. "This is decidedly a miracle", the women said. She came like a divine angel, saved Rajeev for his parents and vanished. "Truly a miracle has saved us from ruin."

On the way back, the children slept. The elders were silent, each evaluating what had happened as per his or her beliefs. "Where could she have gone? It was very remiss of us not to have thanked her even," The ladies berated themselves for the lapse. The men did not have much to say. The whole event had been quite a shock. They were ordinary people with no extraordinary strengths. They were just glad that all were safe. They raced home to the security of their mortgaged houses and struggling businesses.

The crowd was thinning out at the exit to the bridge they had to cross. "What's up," thought Jit as he slowed down. A policeman was asking passersby if they knew anyone with a multi coloured scarf like the one he brandished. Jit pressed on the gas, deciding not to disqualify the Miracle. He had risen above his ordinariness. That was a miracle too.

# The Tango

Their dance was slow, the music was not. Her face was sweating, the rivulets of effort seeping into her blouse and wetting her back. The music was blaring their steps were not. Matching each other, there was a strange rhythm to their quiet movements. They seemed to be stepping only to every second beat of the drums, but they did not miss a step and held their own.

Oblivious to the sudden shift in interest around them, they stepped on, in the joy of their partnership, in the joy of their ability to step in togetherness. Aah! The fun of dancing…Everyone had stopped to look at the pair on the floor. Happiness seemed to flow from each to the other, a passionate embrace that wiped out all previous sorrow, no fearful thoughts of the morrow. After the crescendo, the musicians beat a regretfully slow retreat into silence.

My grandmother at eighty, quite firmly and sensitively led my polio affected daughter of fifteen to a nearby chair, adjusting her long skirt over the Jaipur leg strapped to her thigh. The young one smiled blissful satisfaction at her doting grand mama…the generations had met and there seemed to be no gap there.

# The Baptism

Just before the War in Burma a smaller war happened, with far reaching consequences. Kumari was barely eight years old, when an immense desire took her little imagination by storm. For many days now, she had been watching her friends. Each one wore a white fluffy dress, white netted stockings, white ballet shoes, and white veils covered newly shampooed hair. Some even wore braids of white lilies on their long hair left flowing like the aunties in the magazines she was not allowed to see. She looked yearningly at them.

"I want to do that too", she told herself. "I want to go into the chapel in white, I want to kneel in front of the cage, and say my Holy Mary. I want to come out of the chapel with a new name, just like the others", she decided. The chubby Mother Superior looked benignly at the determined young girl in front of her and relented. "Okay get her ready", was all she said, as she wondered about the ways of God before sending for Kumari's father.

Wearing the pale orange 'Naarumadi', (the holy cloth of the orthodox Tamil Brahman, the huge giant of a man presented himself at the gates of the Convent, where he sent his daughter to study. Every quivering pore of an offended Brahman orthodoxy spewed the burning rays of an angry sun. His bearing was of a stupendously enraged sage. The wrath of an offended patriarch held a halo over his indomitable head.

He stood at the gates, questioning the Mother Superior on her temerity. He challenged her authority to convert his poor misled daughter to the strange customs of an alien religion. Hearing his loud shouts, a shivering waif slowly slunk out, and ran to the protective embrace of her equally fearful mother. The Mother Superior looked on in consternation and wondered.

An air of righteous indignation hung over the Convent Gates, as paternal proprietary rights reclaimed possession of an almost sinner. She had dared to desire to be different. Her punishment would be immediate. He went home and took out her horoscope. He would visit the astrologer the next day and see what her stars foretell. He would arrange to get her married off, as early as possible. Till then she would stay at home and learn to help her mother in the kitchen. Girl children were a burden, in his honest opinion.

Sense of self having been restored, He went back to his prayers and ritualistic obsequies. That was Kumari's Baptism.

# ParimalamPichoo

ParimalamPichoo loved her job. She was a gourmet chef turned travel writer turned author of cookbooks with intriguing recipes. She remembered her first ever such book with great relish. The remote village in the highest reaches of Dhoddabeda Hills had been very invigorating. Their food habits more so and the raw material that went into their cooking was fresh, different, tasty and completely intriguing. They had no equivalent names in English. So, writing that book had been a challenge.

Her next had been culled from the fading memories of a once-upon-a-time cannibal. Her critics called her work gory. However her next book on the eating habits of desert nomads all over the world and the comparative state of their health brought her some glory. She had heard of her present subject at the mountaineering camp for disabled persons. So, here she was. This was going to be more than just a collection of recipes. This was going to be different.

Apprehensively, she opened the gate to the odd looking house at the end of the tree lined avenue. The door was wide open. Hesitating at the door, she slowly entered. She noticed with surprise that the bare wooden sofas were attached to the floor, standing on small rounded concrete cups. "Hellloo", she ventured with alacrity, not sure what the response would be.

A brisk patter of steps heralded the entry of a person with a cane in hand. His vacant looking eyes stopped a few inches above where she stood. He seemed to be listening to her presence in the room. "Yes, please?" His soft seductive voice bowled her over with the pitch and diction. "I'm Parimalam," she stuttered." I heard of this place at the Hillside Camp. Could I talk to Yesudas?" "That's me; would you care to sit here?"

Both sat down and she explained her presence. He smiled slowly, and said, "Sure why not." He led the way to the kitchen, Parimalam following and marvelling at the ease with which he navigated the stairs. He told her not to change the position of anything in the room as he got ready to show her how he cooked. There were very few bottles, and they had labels with protruding pictures and figures. Yesudas was able to run his fingers over them and tell her what was in each one.

With ease born of practice he chopped a few vegetables from the fridge, mixed a batter of gram flour in it, and deep fried fritters for her, in less than fifteen minutes! Soon he had them arranged on a tray, and with two cups of tea on it, he led the way back to the sitting room. Wrapping up her camera and other stuff, Parimalam thanked him profusely for the photo shoot.

"You are only as handicapped as you think yourself to be. Not having sight from birth, I was able to develop a lot of my other sensory perceptions. But even that could not save me from the lorry accidentally hitting me on the footpath. I lost both my legs. Having to adjust to that was a bit tough. I was determined however, to be independent, so I got myself fitted with these fancy crutches, custom made to suit my needs. This house had been built to suit me when I was six feet tall. I would have had to change the whole setup to suit my new height after the accident. So I chose instead to rise to the occasion," he smiled wryly.

"Sometimes I have nightmares of screeching sounds, and searing pain. I wake up sweating and...." He stopped enquiringly at her quick intake of breath. "Oh, I do dream you know." he smiled gently. "Someone once asked me about my dreams. No I do not know what a person looks like but I can feel your looks. My mental picture of what you emote comes to me in my dreams.. When painful or worrisome events occur, I dream of such situations and wake up in fear or dread. Once I dreamt of myself searching for my cane, falling everywhere and hurting my legs. I suddenly woke up remembering I had no legs and cried myself back to sleep." He sounded very matter of fact. No sentimental stuff here.

Any comment she made now would be superfluous. Her eyes were brimming, as she bade goodbye and walked away quickly before he sensed her tears. What an experience she thought to herself as she made her way back to the main road and home. Her perceptions had undergone a sea change. Life had taken on new meaning. She was not going to take any of her blessings for granted, at least for some time more

# *Her Story*

Sanchita collected the soup bowl and the spoon and walked out of the room. She felt very sad. However hard she tried, the food always got thrown out. With a resigned shrug, she walked out to the kitchen. Cleaning up, washing and drying the dishes took an hour.

As the evening wore on, the lights were lit and the drapes drawn. Sanchita spent some time at the computer, surfing. Then, with a huge sigh, she settled down to read aloud to her companion on the bed. She began with Hansel and Gretel, an all time favourite, continued with The Gingerbread Man, and Little Claus and Big Claus. Reading aloud always made her drowsy and she chose her bed time as soon as she could stop.

Morning brought a bright sun peeking shyly from behind the curtains. Sanchita woke with a sigh. She had fixed an appointment with the curator of the museum in the next town. She had to leave early. Mr. Das was a learned man. He had enrolled her in his class on preservation of ancient artefacts. Today, as a special gesture he was to show her how mummies were prepared.

When he saw the light of interest shining from her eyes, he was indulgently amused. "What an interest in the morbid", he thought to himself as she set about preparing the lotions and ointments that he allowed her to use on the tiny dead birds and animals he used as guinea pigs.

Sanchita finished her evening chores in a great hurry as she had important work to do that night. She almost forgot the soup for her silent companion.

Finally when she was ready, she carried her backpack upstairs to the bedroom. Laying it heavily on the side table she prepared for the long evening ahead. She placed all the ointments and lotions and the miles of white lawn fabric in neat piles. Sweetly she called out "Nanny, see what I am going to dress you in. Soon you will be my mummy in every sense of the word".

# A Momentous Decision

The Matrilineal High Command was in its element. Quiet instructions kept being issued from the headquarters in the "ac room", the family living room which was the only one in the house that had any pretensions to modernity. My mother's hands were strengthened by the presence of her maternal aunts, her mother's brothers' wives. The Paternal interest in the ongoing function was stationed near the main door, where the old "dial through the hole" phone had its place.

The guests were expected at four in the evening. Being a Friday, the highly inauspicious 'rahukalam' was in the morning, leaving the evening free for the function. The lists made out from the inner sanctum included specific vegetables and fruits. In the case of the brinjals, even the size, colour and crispness was specified. Fresh flowers from the market were ordered. The betel leaves came in with the Aunts, as their farm in Trichinopoly had acres of betel leaf creepers. What could be more auspicious than that? Even Lakshmi the white and brown jersey cow was brought in early from her grassy walkabout to be milked of the freshest milk for the coffee.

The general air of anticipation around the house permeated the girls' chambers nearer the back of the house. Frantic last minute efforts were being made to pass off my buxom cousin in as reasonably thin attire as possible. It was hoped she would look thinner in silks. A chiffon sari over satin underskirts, in none too light a colour, with vertical lines did the trick. She at once seemed taller and slimmer. The appetizing smells of semolina halwa and freshly fried brinjal and raw plantain fritters teased the nostrils. The strong aroma of filter coffee brewing in the huge brass filters had its own "axe" appeal.

At the appointed time, the taxi drew to a stop outside the gates. A jumble of people tumbled out and organized themselves for an "entry". The father led the way in followed by the mother, her eldest son and his wife and a scrawny lad of fifteen drew his youngest uncle into the house. Introductions over, the "girl to be seen" was sent for. She came in, and a round of questions followed. She had glared her dissension when asked to fall at the feet of the visitors. When pressed, she sang a light song praising Lord Muruga took small peeks at the groom while handing out the coffee, and was quietly ushered back to her room.

Rajan had "seen" the girl for all of ten minutes. His family noted that she had a nice soft voice. She did not trip over her sari, so she was used to wearing it at home. She did display her annoyance with her expressive eyes. That could be forgiven, as she was convent educated. Well, her weight could be an issue. Rajan's family lived on the second floor of a building that had no lifts. His mother was sure that the problem of weight would be addressed over time. Her father passed his opinion on the culinary skills of the ladies of her house. The coffee was very good, he opined. The uncle who had brokered the match had already assured them of a good dowry, a fashionable wedding and an abundance of electronic and electrical appliances needed for setting up of a new family in their house.

The lucky postman received a generous baksheesh for bringing the post card that declared Rajan's amicable disposition toward the marriage. Would the girl's family now proceed in the matter?

# The Divine Comedy

"This could not be happening to me," thought Srila as she looked on what could only be called a divine comedy. Divine, because only God in His wisdom could have seen fit to let her see it. It was a comedy because, what was going on there was too preposterous to be called anything else. Shri was nearly twenty years older than that chit of a girl. Surely he had never displayed any lack of interest in herself that should have aroused her suspicions. Even the "Best Matched Couple of the Year Cup" had not lost its sheen in its place in the glass cupboard.

So, how could this be? Just How? Dear God in heaven, he seemed fairly smitten even at this distance. They were walking hand in hand and pausing every so often to hold hands and gaze over the placid waters of the lake. They seemed to be drawing closer with every pause.

"...and the meeting dragged on for ages. I have not been able to finish my regular work, so I shall be late getting back. Wait dinner for me. Let's have dinner together, okay?" Shri loosened his tie as he laid the phone back on its cradle. "Better get through this last batch of files," he thought as he settled down to a couple of hours of brow-knitted concentration.

As he let himself into the flat at nine thirty, he gave a lopsided grin, mouthed sorry to his wife and headed straight to the bedroom for a bath and a change of clothes, before dinner. He studied her serene looks as she served dinner and congratulated himself for a calm and composed wife. Their after-dinner chat was a ritual, as it helped him to unwind and her to talk of her day too. Settling down for the night, Shri marvelled at her simplistic outlook on life, her trust and blind faith in him. Far from making him feel ashamed, he blamed her naiveté for his interest in the raunchy Regina and temperamental Taara. "Life is being good to me," he sighed in contentment while gentle snores announced his retirement to the night.

The next day dawned bright and sunny. Finishing her chores early Srila prepared for her day's outing by packing a sandwich along with her video camera and zoom lens in a handy carry bag. Humming softly, she swung her jaunty way to the nature park, where she had seen her husband the previous day. She took up her place behind the huge Banyan tree just outside the Nature Park and settled down to wait.

That evening, he called to say that he was at the gymkhana and in the midst of a game of bridge with some office friends. "I'll be late again, but dinner as usual. Okay? Just wear your pink salwar. I'll bring you your favourite jasmines. I Love you," his voice caressed as he hung up on her. Shri spent just five minutes mentally relishing his outing with Regina at the cottage in the nature park, before settling down with his office work. This damned thing had to be done and ready for his secretary or the workplace would suffer. He would have to make unnecessary explanations. Shri liked his life without too many complications.

Waking up early was not new to Srila. Her brisk good morning at six only drew a moan of protest from him, promptly followed by snuggling deeper into the blanket. The buzz of activity in the hall and kitchen however brought Shri with a quizzical frown to the bedroom door. Srila looked up brightly from her polishing and vacuuming. With a bright smile she wished him a Happy Birthday.

"Come back early from office today. We are having a party at six in the evening. Bring your friends if you want," she offered generously.

By evening their two families had arrived and helped her with the finishing touches to the carefully planned menu. When Shri arrived with Regina and Taara and two other young men in tow, Srila nodded in grim satisfaction. She set herself to be a charming and considerate hostess. The Best Matched Couple of the Year Cup had its pride of place on the table, with all the food set around it. Dinner was a rocking meal with a lot of Oohs and Aahs, and dessert was declared Delicious by one and all.

The time of reckoning had come. She was more composed than ever before. "Surprise, surprise" said Srila as she got the Television set ready and inserted the Video in its slot. The film roll'd and toll'd..

# The Stone on the Road

The stone was an irksome bit of masonry thrown negligently on a part of the road near the kerb. The kerb was hidden under mountains of debris thrown by irresponsible builders in the neighbourhood. A lot of patchwork and repair was going on in three buildings so much so that the area looked like a war zone. It was funny to see the labourers wearing tin helmets as they went about their work. The men women and children who scurried on their way to varying destinations however were as protected or unprotected as their prayers to a distant unseen deity allowed.

The stone which occupied less than a square foot of territory was indeed well used. Little children scampering park ward stepped over it in a ritualistic game. Older folks with greater wisdom stepped round it. Those who saw it too late in their preoccupied perambulations however suffered the ignominy of caring clucks of voiceless chiding from their companions. Some tripped, doddered and straightened up in three or four quickly corrective steps.

The youth of course had his/her own way of handling it. Almost all of them conversed animatedly into their cell phones or listened to the latest filmy numbers on i-pods.

As they reached the object of our concentrated study, some would lightly skip over it while others would abstractedly kick at it as if at a football. They would then hop a bit to ease the pain and move on. A million other activities drew them away from the scene.

The pretty young thing and her chivalrous attendant stopped at the stone. "How negligent can people be; leaving a stone this size in the middle of the road" she opined. That worthy, immediately responded by bending down to move it to the side. The tight jeans he wore did not help him to stoop low enough and laughing, he self consciously abandoned the task.

A young diffident girl in a very colourful salwar kameez and carrying a fancy bag was the next. She was perhaps very aware in every pore of her body of the huge hulk walking beside her. She did not see the stone until she literally tripped and fell. Deftly sticking his left hand out he stopped her halfway and steadied her with his right. Something beautiful happened between them. Two pairs of shy eyes flew to meet each other locked endearingly and tore away in confusion. One pair in seemly modesty refused to look up and the other pair in proud self praise did not look down. Instead it looked round to see who had witnessed the incident.

Quickly I drew the curtains to save them embarrassment and almost toppled my old house owner who had been standing behind me and watching the scene. She chuckled conspiratorially." Five years back, the same happened to me.

That was the only time in forty five years that my husband touched me in public. Those two are to be engaged. Mark my words. They will marry and live happily ever after" she said laughingly and went away.

All for a torn bit of masonry

# Vedanayaki

*This story has to begin at the very beginning. When Vedanayaki was summoned to the front room, she had no inkling of the portentous happenings that would change her life. Her ten year old intelligence sufficed her to worry whether her brother would change the position of her coin on the game of ludo that she had left behind. Wiping her chalk dusted hands on her skirts; she entered the Study in some perturbation. She could see her father's assistant hovering over the huge desk adorning the western corner. Hovering meant that her father was in a tizzy and that was not a good sign.*

Having been seen however, she had no choice but to hang on to her mother's sari and hope that her irate father would send her back to her games soon enough. He looked her up and down, as if examining what she would look like in a few years. "Obey your mother when the time comes," he admonished, without offering an explanation for his words. She looked at her mother, bristling in silent protest and saw her smile comfortingly at her. She seemed to be saying that it did not matter. "Can I go play now?" Her query earned a frown from her already upset father. Her mother however shooed her away, and she gladly ran into the dark and cool interiors.

Her parents were talking seriously. Rather, her father was. He issued terse commands and her mother listened dutifully, her nine-yard sari draped elegantly around her slight frame. She made note of all his instructions and sighed. "Can we not wait another year or two? She has just attained puberty. You know that too." He looked at her in an unblinkingly suppressive stare. All further arguments were effectively squashed. She moved herself quietly away.

The wedding was conducted with great pomp and pleasure. The groom's family was well represented: the empty boxes of Ovaltine in the dustbin were proof of that. The whole village estimated the length of the used plantain leaves dotting the rubbish heap. They counted the number of sweets thrown carelessly out in the leafy remains. They nodded their heads in collective pride and some individual envy, and they seemed to say, "Shri certainly has done his daughter proud". Furtive feminine glances at the boy's side of the hall however drew slightly sharp breaths and dismayed coughs. He was old! He was at least twenty years older. Their in-drawn breaths caused their breasts to heave and sway. They felt a personal loss. A sense of frustrated helplessness permeated their very beings. The festivities went on of their own volition. Those who had come for the enjoyment, enjoyed. Those who were there out of camaraderie for the bride, chaffed at their inability to protest. The more philosophically inclined just shrugged their shoulders. It was a father's prerogative to choose his daughter's husband. The food was good. It quickly coated the few consciences that ticked uncomfortably at the mismatch and the musicians from the city played very well.

Veda's painful entry into the rituals of marital fulfilment did not douse her interest in her games. Her nine yard sari notwithstanding, she continued to play hopscotch with her younger sibling. The chores she had to undertake in the kitchen were a different kettle of fish altogether. She learned to cut vegetables without shedding her youthful blood. She could make mouth- watering dishes by the end of the first year, all on her own. The wood stove was a tear wrencher and she shed copious amounts of that when her mother would not let her go without learning how to handle it. Veda loved her music lessons and found refuge in singing whenever she had the time. Her father, a pedagogue at heart, undertook to teach her the nuances of the English language and encouraged her to read. The auspicious day for her entry into her husband's home was drawing near. She sensed a sort of caring energy in her mother. A lot of new clothes were bought; jewels and silverware were burnt with her initials, weighed and listed. In her twelve years of life what fond memory would she take, to cherish and nurture in her new home? At last she was ready to leave.

Vedanayaki felt no compunction at having to go. She was told that there would be young kids her age. She looked forward to playing games with them. Her own preparation for her life's journey consisted of searching and stocking on smooth round pebbles to play with and flat pieces of stone that could be used to play hopscotch... She remembered to fill her draw- string purse with small cowrie shells which would help her win in dice games. Not for the world would she be separated from them. In the one year since her marriage she had grown into a strapping young girl. Her height and weight were elegantly distributed and she looked handsome in her nice new nine-yard sari. With a string of jasmines in her hair, she jumped gaily onto the horse cart that had been ordered for her.

## *That was then. This was now.*

She remembered with a wan smile her reception at the station. The nearly middle aged man who came to the station to meet her had a pronounced limp. He had seemed old from her breezy twelve year old stance. She looked at him with sympathy and promised herself she would be kind to him. He registered her friendly smile with a frown and a scowl. Collecting her luggage from the attendants who had come with her, the limping stranger moved ahead without inviting them to his house. A sudden cold breeze blew her composure to shivering smithereens. She hurried forward to keep pace with her host. In the melee of the hurrying passengers she got separated from the rest of her people from home and was hustled into a waiting horse cart. This one was well decorated. The jingle of bells that shook the horse's head made her feel welcome in a way nothing else did.

She remembered her shock when on reaching her new home she realized that the stranger who had brought her home was in fact her husband. Her initiation into housewifely services started with a bang, when the children of his first wife, two sons aged five and seven rushed into the room and dragged her off to play. Barely twelve, she found herself mothering them as best she could. They perhaps found a kindred spirit in her enthusiastic responses to their overtures of friendship. Their grandmother, her husband's mother, her mother in law, had been very accommodating. At first she trained her well in the skills needed to run her husband's home. Amma took care of the boys. As fate would have it, amma died the following year after a bad bout of cholera. At the very young age of fourteen Veda found herself with the task of looking to the needs of her family.

Managing the kitchen was fine. Managing her step sons was also fine. The proximity in their ages helped build a deep bond with them in the formative years of their relationship. It was when she was fifteen that her husband made his first advance to satisfy his carnal needs. She remembered the first time with great shivering sobs. She had contracted a fever that had cooled his ardour for a few days. He had tasted pleasure, and he was not to be denied for long. Soon she had accepted her lot with stoic submission. She however just could not change her mental rejection of his physical deformity. Slowly she learned to use her charms to bargain for her rights and needs. She looked on him with pity for being such a wimp that he would marry one as young as her. Veda's feelings for her father hardened to one of polished distaste. He had chosen this monster for her? Growing out of her teens, she looked more and more regal. She took to wearing elaborate hairdos whenever she went out of the house. Her saris were very colourful and her lips stained betel-red, drew the attention of everyone who saw her. The male neighbours jumped up to serve her every wish and she responded by presenting them with delicious stuff to eat.

Her husband saw all this with great disquiet. He did not have the guts to ask her anything. He was aware in every pore of his body that she loathed him. By that curious chemistry which keeps such couples going, their marriage also thrived, overtly. Covertly however small changes occurred within the house. He took to sleeping in the drawing room. His massive study table where he wrote his theses on every philosophy under the sun was moved into the shaded part of the balcony. A small folding table too was set up ostensibly to enable him to eat as he worked. It now transpired that he had his meals in royal solitude. More often than not food started appearing in hot cases that were left on the table much before time. He had to serve himself. He found it easier to finish dinner in the college canteen before setting out to the house. At least it saved him the bother of clearing the table at night. His sleep was disturbed by the situation in which he found himself. He wondered what course his future would take. He made no effort to change his plight. He would shrug the academic bent of his studious shoulders to indicate that what was destined would not be denied.

On the home front Veda had found a great camaraderie growing between her husband's two sons and herself. She ceased to wonder at the strange quirk of fate that had given her sons, just a few years younger than her. She had ceased to think of the effect her wantonness was having on her husband, now too old to be able to handle her youthful needs. Her lack of formal education was being made up with life lessons from her sons. She was increasingly thankful to them for that. They were close enough to each other for the boys to feel the injustice that had been done to their step mother, but they were conditioned to not questioning. Their father had been as strict with them at home as he was with his students at college. They chose to go with the tide and enjoy the company of their youthful and handsome young stepmother. They got a kick out of introducing her to their friends, as their mother. She looked so young, vibrant and lovely.

One fine evening, after a riotous party at their friend's house the two boys returned home to find the whole place in disarray. Books had been thrown about. Their father's cane had been broken in two. There was a sound of huge moaning from the kitchen. Deep sobs rent the air interspersed with hard words and curses aimed at their father. The two of them tip toed into the kitchen with great trepidation, not knowing what they would find. Seeing them Veda rose with a cry and ran towards them. Harish the younger felt very awkward not knowing what to say. He busied himself cleaning the mess before slowly tripping quietly out of the flat.

"He called me Wanton" she whimpered. "He beat me with his stick and I pulled it out of his hand and gave him a couple of thwacks", she continued with grim joy. The "he' was nowhere to be seen, so Rudra took it upon himself to console her. He made her some tea and sat next to her while she drank. "Okay, so what made you fight?" He queried delicately, wanting to and yet again not really wanting to know. She set the tea tumbler on the floor and went to the shelf near the door. "Actually it looked so colourful in its packets, swinging in the breeze that I just had to buy a couple. The shop keeper from whom I buy my betel leaves smiled in a strange way when I asked for it," she complained. "See, I only showed this to your dad and he set on me like a caged tiger let loose". In her outstretched hand lay two pouches of a very potent blend of flavoured tobacco. Her husband had responded to this misdemeanour with so much rage? A slight shiver ran up her spine.

The serious looking tailor in the fourth block of flats had told her he would show her some movies on his home projector. She had gone there on Saturday. They had seen snippets from some old black and white movies. He had laughed a lot at all of her jokes. They had shared a very nice evening before home duties had pulled her away. She wondered now what her husband would do if she told him about that evening. Actually she would have spoken of it earlier but she had felt a great thrill at being able to hide it from him. In fact she savoured the sensations that had risen in her heart at the thought of a sweet friendship. She did not want to share it with anyone; not even her sons. The tailor had even held his hand over hers at the lift door. She recalled the sudden movement of some swift pain in her loins. At night, since then, she tried to duplicate that intenseness by concentrating deeply to recall every moment before that feeling rose. Frustratingly she was not very successful and waited in agony for the next time she would be called over for a visit.

Meanwhile matters at home limped back to normalcy. The boys had finished one set of exams and were waiting for their results. Rudra would be leaving for Bombay to do his internship for a two month period at a foundry there. Harish would then have to be the care taker for his young and beautiful mother. He would have to go between mom and dad, as neither of them deigned to talk to each other. He would have to do the fetching and the carrying from the markets. He really felt awkward with her these days. He could not concentrate on his studies either. The scent of her bath soap lingered in his thoughts much longer than was necessary. He could tell in which part of the house she was and what she was doing by just listening to her footfalls and the tinkle of her anklets. They were the same silver anklets that he and Rudra had gifted her on her twentieth birthday. She had been greatly thrilled then. Those silvery sounds kept him awake at night now, as he strained his ears to guess whether she was asleep or not. Imagination built verily on his own knowledge of her and gained monstrously in his fevered manifestation of his importance to her.

## *Life had moved on like the Juggernaut.*

In the course of the first ten years of his second marriage Parthiban swung like a drunken pendulum between the two extremes of hope and despair, fear and bravado, philosophical acceptance and unbridled passion. He had allowed himself to be talked into this unacceptable situation. He had acted on an impulse and allowed the first alliance brought to his notice. His mother had been in a hurry, perhaps she was afraid he would change his mind and refuse to remarry. He was steeped in his research work at the University. His great interest in philosophy and the ancient languages had got him a well paying job. For him work came first. After his rejected overtures, he found it easy to divert himself with work, and more work.

The first time he tried to touch her was etched in his tortured mind. The day had been warm and sweaty from early in the morning. She had been wearing a lovely green coloured sari. The nine yards swathed round her lissom body had stirred forgotten memories within him. She had lost the game of ludo to Rudra and was being petulant. He had been teasing her. She had made such lovely moue with her red lips that he had found himself staring at her every reaction. He had gone closer and placed a hand on her shoulders. The fierce hell cat that wailed like a banshee had frozen his libido in a grotesque and comic whimper that just dribbled and frothed out of the side of his shivering mouth.

After a couple of years when she had grown to accept him with some kind of resignation, he had approached the topic foremost on his mind. His desire to have her bear his third child was met with a certain disregard. Her look of utter disdain and absolute revulsion had cast him into a deep well of depression. So he had retired hurt, keeping a wary eye on her activities and yearning for the comfort and fulfilment that only she could give him. He had wished himself to be the recipient of any kind of interest from her. He had even prayed to all the gods his mother had introduced him to. Nothing had helped, until he got a work order for a new research project, and that had saved him.

His ardour had cooled. He had conditioned himself to live his life without expectations. He controlled his thirsty senses by observing every penance possible. He ate the food cooked by her with great concentration. Her beautiful hands had touched every morsel that he chewed. So what if she would not touch him? He took to using scraps of material from her used saris as towels to cover his pillow when he slept. The reason he said was to keep the pillow from getting oily. He however loved the residual scent of his woman on the cloth, which he inhaled deeply as he slept. He yearningly watched her napping in the huge wooden swing in the afternoons, her sari attractively awry. He however maintained his distance until she beckoned, which was not very often, and on those days he was given sight of a distant heaven, soon over.

He watched with amazement at the rather quick way in which she had adjusted to his home town and his schedules. He was jealous of his sons for the wonderful relationship that they shared with their mother. He was envious of the people who came in touch with her. Later he noticed that she touched quite a few of the people she came across. He had no way of telling her to be careful of strangers. The ridicule and loathing she felt for him would surface and scorch him in its intensity. None of the three worlds he read of, had a sun as scorching as her looks when her anger against him was roused. He patiently and humbly acknowledged to himself that she looked beautiful even then.

He strove to please her at every point. Her every wish was his command. He wanted to befriend this little wife of his with every honourable husband-ly intention. He found some solace in the disciplines imposed on him by his rigorous study and practice of the scriptures. That study helped him cope. He was conditioned to not provoking. He was educated in the ways of introspection. He hoped he would be able to find solutions to the situations he was facing. Mental peace and harmony was his motive. All turbulence in life slowly evaporates in time. That is what his holy texts promised. What his philosophies could not do however was to smooth the feverish anticipation of a sex starved body. Would mind win over matter? He started a new batch of penances to appease the angry gods and ease his tortured psyche. That was when he spotted her.

She had tasted and enjoyed the scented tobacco powder in her betel leaves. She had laughingly addressed the kiosk owner. That kiosk was eminently viewable from his study window. She had bought her betel leaves and a couple of tamil magazines, when another person moved into view. The tailor was making hugely flattering gestures in a familiar way. She had slowly succumbed to his insistence and had allowed him to pay for her purchases. He had given her a gift of some silvery thing. She had accepted the gift and thanked him gaily. "What could it mean? Was this enticement or payment?" Jealousy has neither caste nor creed. Nor is it peculiar to the moneyed class. It has only colour...a blazing hot white or a blazing hot red. It had the power to annihilate.

He had had a raving temper tantrum. She had effectively silenced him by breaking his own walking stick on his back. In anger and shame he had walked out of the house. Where could he go? After a few hours of cooling his heels in the unfriendly stares of the neighbours and townspeople alike, he returned home to silence and resentful glances from the three of them. After a few days, things returned to a fair amount of normalcy. Battle lines were smudged if not wholly erased. Lunch and dinner started smelling as delicious as before. His clothes resumed a well cared sheen. His shoes were placed facing the door every morning. The new walking stick mocked him with its newness. His friends declared him lucky for having a wife who would gift him such a lovely staff. His friends enviously said that they would have been beaten, not gifted.

In the first few days after Rudra left he found Harish more and more at home. On being questioned about college and attendance penalties, he would evade his questions and pretend to study.

## *Harish and Rudra*

Harish found it hard to concentrate on his books. He took to stealing old playboy magazines from the waiting room of his friend's father who had a poly clinic. The tone and selection of his reading choices shifted. Parthiban watched quietly, gauging his son's mood swings. Some days he seemed to be high strung. Some days he was very disturbed. He would not sit still for a moment and would stomp out of the house if reprimanded. There were days when he would entertain all with his wit and some when he would lounge about mooning and sighing like a heroine from the films of yesteryear. As expected, Harish failed his second year exams and was permitted to continue to the next year's course with a strict injunction that he would make a successful effort in the mid-term examination opportunity offered for failed students. Parthiban took it on himself to coach his son and do his duty by him.

One evening after an excessively discordant session with his harsh and demanding father, Harish left home for a turn in the park nearby. He was realizing with a degree of self denouncement, his attraction for his step mother. Her presence in the room when he studied turned him to jelly. He found himself regarding jealously, the people who received her attentions in the neighbourhood. He loathed the tailor most of all. He thought him to be coarse and lecherous. His toothy smiles and habit of being at the petty shop every time his mother was there upset him. He found himself blaming his father for being less than manly. He found reason to blame everything under the sun on the orthodox conditioning of their collective upbringing. He was dying to break out of the bonds of confounding resentment that held him in confusion. He did not know how.

That was when the incident with his parents had happened. He had been happy that his father had expressed himself in a suitably forceful manner. When he heard from his brother what had caused the tantrum however, his venomous moods found a different outlet. He took to stalking the tailor stealthily at first and more openly later. His unbridled passions and disturbing emotions led him through the dark alleys of drugs and drink.

The inevitable happened one evening, when in an inebriated state he willed his unsatisfied desires on his mother. The tempest that followed the event destroyed all in its path. The tragedy was witnessed by that hapless harbinger of disaster, his father. In morbid fear of his own life he could do nothing but dither and dally.

He dared not shout for fear of the neighbours knowing his shame. He was not strong enough to stand up to his strapping young son. He was mortally afraid. He was also overcome with shame at his own feebleness. What could he do? He prayed incoherently and fell into a deep swoon. Disgusted with his act on realizing the enormity of his crime, Harish walked out of the flat saying sorry over and over again.

Vedanayaki fought to control her feelings. On one level she was disgusted, cheapened, sullied like never before. She bathed her hurt person and persona, using coconut roughage to brush off the vestiges of the assault. She felt she had been used like a sponge and discarded. She bent her head in shame. She should have anticipated this. She should have known the signs of his discomfort. If only she had not been so involved with the tailor, matters would not have come to such a sordid pass. Poor Harish, she felt his pain. Her feeling of revulsion at his act was not greater than her love for him as a youngster in her care. If only...if only...went her mind. If only she had taken note of Harish earlier, she could have satiated his need and educated him the way she had done Rudra. She was conditioned to the vagaries of the chauvinists who manipulated her stars. She felt personally responsible for the tragedy.